KW-487-350

Our Strangers

LYDIA DAVIS

CANONGATE

This book will ONLY be available at independent bookstores, libraries and Bookshop.org

This paperback edition published in 2024 by Canongate Books

First published in Great Britain in 2023 by Canongate Books Ltd,
14 High Street, Edinburgh EH1 1TE

canongate.co.uk

1

This is a work of fiction. All of the characters, organisations and events portrayed are either products of the author's imagination or are used fictitiously.

Copyright © 2023, Lydia Davis

The right of Lydia Davis to be identified as the author of this work has been asserted by her in accordance with the Copyright, Designs and Patents Act 1988

Excerpt from *The Granite Pail: The Selected Poems of Lorine Niedecker* published by North Point Press, 1985. Copyright © 1985 by the Estate of Lorine Niedecker. By permission of Bob Arnold, Literary Executor for the Estate of Lorine Niedecker.

Every effort has been made to trace copyright holders and obtain their permission for the use of copyright material. The publisher apologises for any errors or omissions and would be grateful if notified of any corrections that should be incorporated in future reprints or editions of this book.

British Library Cataloguing-in-Publication Data
A catalogue record for this book is available on request from the British Library

ISBN 978 1 80530 219 3

Book design by Jordan Koluch

Printed and bound by CPI Group (UK) Ltd, Croydon CR0 4YY

FSC
www.fsc.org
MIX
Paper | Supporting responsible forestry
FSC® C171272

Our Strangers is available for sale only at physical bookshops, Bookshop.org, and selected online independent retailers. Davis is deeply concerned about monopolistic bookselling, and hopes this decision will both stand as a sign of her solidarity with independent booksellers and encourage further conversation about the vital importance of a diverse publishing ecosystem.

Contents

I

II

III

IV

V

I

My Briefcase

Obviously, it was because of my briefcase that they hired me to teach again the following term. They were impressed because my briefcase looked so much like a briefcase.

I also knew how to walk down the halls and carry my briefcase. I could unlock my office door and walk into my office. I had a swivel chair on wheels in my office. I left my door open during my office hour and closed it firmly the moment the office hour was over. The department secretary did anything I asked her to, within reason. I was careful about what I asked her to do. I was brisk and preoccupied in front of her, but with a polite smile. There was my mailbox, with my name on it in bold letters, below the clock. Also, I spoke to a student, when I met one in the hallway, with the correct expression, a little dazed and distracted, but my answers were always clear and final.

On Sufferance

The cat says, "I'm only here on sufferance." The dog doesn't understand, so the cat defines the word *sufferance*. It has to do with a kind of tolerance. It has to do with permission that is only indirect, permission through failure to prohibit. She uses the word *tacit*. The dog doesn't understand *tacit*. The cat gives up. She thinks he probably got the idea anyway.

The cat knows they love the dog and merely tolerate her. There is real enthusiasm when they greet the dog, when they come in the front door. She sits off in the background, watching, because the dog is so wild when he jumps on them. They see her in the background and say, "Hello, kitty!" but without much warmth. The dog is more demonstrative than she is. He wouldn't understand the word *demonstrative*, though he enacts it. (He wouldn't understand the word *enact*.)

Later, the cat says to the dog, who stands below her, in the kitchen, watching her and sniffing the air, "Now she has left the room and I'm sitting up here within an inch of her chicken sandwich. That puts a strain on me." She reaches out a forepaw and touches the sandwich, but she is not comfortable.

The dog likes her and is interested in her. Although he doesn't know the word *strain*, he would not find it a strain to be near the chicken sandwich.

Then she says she has trouble with her salivary glands in certain situations and can't help opening and closing her mouth.

Later the cat is chewing on the broom again.

The dog does not understand why she would do that.

The cat says, "She scolds me because I've been chewing on the broom. She leaves it out and I see it. Then she sees me chewing on it and comes and puts it away between the refrigerator and the wall where I can't get at it, though I try. I try when it seems to be where I can reach it."

The dog listens to her explain all this. At least it is a change from going back to sleep again in that pool of sunlight, as he has been doing from time to time all morning, as it shifts across the floor.

Just a Little

Agnes Varda, the French film director,
said in an interview
that she liked to do a little sewing,
a little cooking, a little gardening, a little baby care—
but just a little.

The Stages of Womanhood

It was in the midst of these days when I was struggling to complete the—what would it be?—seventh, no, sixth stage of my growth as a woman, being a year late already with that, according to the (ineffective) anthroposophic doctor I had consulted about my persistent ear infections, when I was awoken yet again during a particularly restless night of being awoken, first, by my child, then by a mosquito, then by my child again, then by the tickling in my ears, then by my child again—when I was awoken yet again, this time by the high-pitched wail of an air-raid siren that I mistook at first for a malfunctioning fan in one window and then a fan in another, going around turning off and unplugging the fans one by one, then finally making my way downstairs and out the back door to stand in the yard looking up until the sound of the siren died abruptly, the wail descending. Of course I thought of war, since our country was in conflict yet again with another country. I thought maybe the mosquito that had been bothering me would live longer than I would. I thought of calling the local police station. I wondered if my husband had heard the siren through his ear plugs. He was sleeping downstairs so that he would not be bothered by me, since I was sleeping so badly these days, or by the child, who was waking so often. The doctor had told me that the next stage, the last stage of womanhood in which a woman is reproductive, was very important creatively. The stage that came after that was very different—also wonderful, she said, but very different. But I had not yet completed this stage, which was supposed to be a growth into full womanhood. As far as I could see, I was exactly the same this year as I had been last year and the year before.

A Brief News Story from Long Ago

We heard this story years ago on the evening news: a bride and groom on their wedding night did some heavy drinking with friends and then got into the bride's car and drove away. In a dead-end road near an overpass, they stopped the car, turned off the engine, and began to argue loudly. The argument was audible to the houses nearby and went on for so long that several neighbors began to listen. After a while, the groom shouted to his bride, "All right, run over me then." By now, the neighbors were also watching out their windows. He left the car, slamming the door behind him, and lay down in front of the front wheel on the passenger side. The bride started the car and drove the 4,000-pound vehicle over him. He died instantly. The marriage was only a few hours old. At the time of his death, he was still wearing his tuxedo.

Fear of Loose Tongue

Please be kind, Ron, she says.
No mention of *anything*
that may or may not have occurred
at Hamburger Mary's!

Caramel Drizzle

"Caramel syrup or caramel drizzle?"

"Sorry?"

"Caramel syrup or caramel drizzle?"

This is overheard conversation. I look up: it is a tall slim woman with a ponytail buying the drink at a Starbucks counter. She is wearing a dark blue uniform. We are in an airport. She is probably a flight attendant.

Long pause for deliberation. She has not encountered this choice before.

"I'll take the drizzle."

Now I see her from behind, over there, with her blond ponytail and sticking-out ears, drinking her caramel drizzle.

While she stood at the counter and deliberated, I was deciding that the drizzle was a smaller amount of caramel than the syrup, even though surely syrup must be involved in the drizzle.

Later, she walks away with another airline employee, the empty cup in her hand, the caramel drizzle inside her.

And then she turns out to be the attendant on my flight—her name is Shannon. So, her caramel drizzle will also be going with us to Chicago.

The Talk Artist

His literary form is the live talk, without notes, without script. After he has given them, these talks may be published. Now I am reading a talk he has given in Philadelphia—the words are there on the page, and I hear him speaking them, though I don't know him or the sound of his voice. I am reading this in the bath, and even if I weren't in the bath, I would find there was a certain intimacy in reading something written by someone who cares about writing, especially a talk he once delivered in person.

Then I am at a party, and I see the author of the talk. He leans across several people to shake hands with me, clutching with his other hand the two lapels of his corduroy jacket and smiling with the friendliness of someone who has just arrived at a party, but not speaking. He doesn't speak, and all evening I am not within earshot of him and don't see him speaking, so for me, for that part of the evening, he remains speechless. But back at home, the book still lies open over the rim of the bathtub, and in it, though a little less friendly than in person, a little more serious, he is speaking at great length and without interruption.

The Other She

From where she is, in another part of the house, she hears his voice in the bedroom, in the distance, speaking gently, domestically, thoughtfully to her. He does not know she is not in the room.

And for a moment, then, she feels there is another she, with him, maybe even a better she, and that she herself is a spurned she, a scorned she, there at the end of the hall, far away from the room where they have something nice going on together.

Everyone Used to Cry

It is not easy to live in this world: everyone is upset constantly by the large or even small things that go wrong. One is insulted by a friend, another is neglected by her family, yet another has a bad argument with his spouse or teenage child.

Often, people cry when they are unhappy. This is natural. For a year or so, when I was young, I worked in an office. Toward lunchtime, as the people in the office grew hungry and tired and irritable, they would begin to cry. My boss would give me a document to type, and I would push it away crossly. He would yell at me, "Type it!" I would yell back, "I won't!" He himself would become petulant on the phone and slam it into its cradle. By the time he was ready to leave for lunch, tears of frustration would be running down his cheeks. If an acquaintance stopped in at the office to take him to lunch, he would ignore that person, and turn his back. Then that person's eyes, too, would well up with tears.

After lunch, we all felt better, and the office was filled with its normal hum and bustle, people carrying folders and walking briskly here and there, sudden bursts of laughter rising from cubicles, and work would go well until late in the afternoon. Then, as we all grew tired again, even more tired than in the morning, and hungry again, we would begin crying again.

Most of us actually continued to cry as we left the office. In the elevator, we would push one another aside, and on the walk to the subway we would glare at the people coming toward us. On the stairs descending into the subway, we would force our way down through the crowd coming up.

It was summer. In those days there was no air-conditioning in the subway cars, and while the tears wet our cheeks, the sweat also ran down our faces, backs, and legs, and the women's feet swelled in their tight shoes, as we all stood packed together, swaying between stops.

Some people, though they were crying when they got into the subway car, would gradually stop crying as they rode toward home, especially if they had found a seat. They would blink their damp eyelashes and begin contentedly biting on their knuckles as they read their newspapers and books, their eyes still shining.

They might not cry again that day, not until the next day. I don't know, because I wasn't with them, I can only imagine. I myself would not usually cry at home, except at the table, if my supper was very disappointing, or close to bedtime, because I did not really want to go to bed, because I did not want to get up the next day and go to work. But maybe others did cry at home, maybe even all evening, depending on what they found there.

Father Has Something to Tell Me

Father stands in the kitchen and tries to explain to me something about Christianity. But I've had another long day, I'm tired, I'm not listening, and he can see that I'm not listening. Later he goes upstairs and types out a two-paragraph statement clarifying what he was trying to explain to me earlier. Before he brings it to me, he shows it to Mother for her comments. I figure this out later, because I remember hearing his footsteps over my head going into her bedroom, the silence while she reads what he has written, and then the rumble of their voices. He comes down to where I am now, in the living room, and hands me the typed statement. He says that of course I don't have to read it right away.

A Moment Long Ago: The Itinerant Photographer

An itinerant photographer has set up his camera, lights, and chair in a local grocery store. This was many years ago. I was there, I saw it myself. A very small girl is sitting in the chair, hardly more than a baby. He is having a hard time with her. She will not smile. She watches him solemnly. At last, in desperation, he holds up an orange giraffe, takes a step toward her, and waves it wildly in her face. At that, she opens her mouth wide, showing her two lower teeth, her only teeth, and bursts into tears.

Claim to Fame #2: Karl Marx and My Father

Karl Marx and my father both had daughters. Both daughters grew up to become translators. Both translated Gustave Flaubert's *Madame Bovary*!

The Joke

When the straitlaced brothers dropped by, churchgoers Larry and Averill Knickerbocker, to give us their bills, I was embarrassed by the state of the house—the kitchen they walked into from the porch, and the living room, the two places they would see. Clothes and toys strewn everywhere. Stains on the cabinet doors. Dishes piled on the counters and in the sink. The high chair tray sticky. It was no excuse that I was a tired young mother, helping to support us all and taking care of the house as best I could. And now the baby's father and I were talking about a separation.

Larry needed a pen to write something on his bill. I gave him a pen that was lying on the kitchen table and walked into the living room with Averill to show him the ceiling.

Later, when they were gone, I looked at the bill, which we would now be able to pay. We had had no money at all, just $42 in our savings account, and then my husband's father had died—suddenly, out of the blue. He was a bachelor and a bit of a rake. My husband had gone down to New Jersey and sold his Cadillac and come home with a check for $10,000.

I looked at the door they had gone out of, and the empty driveway where their truck had been parked. Then I picked up the pen and looked at it.

Printed on the pen was a joke: "What's the difference between parsley and pussy? You don't eat parsley."

I laughed so hard, then—not at the joke, really, more at the joke plus the situation—that the baby, off in the next room, started laughing too.

We had probably taken the pen with us from my father-in-law's house when we were cleaning it out.

But later, I thought: I don't know about other people, but I know that we do eat parsley.

Fear of Aging

At twenty-eight,
she longs to be twenty-five again.

Addie and the Chili

Years ago, Ellie asked me to write the story of our friend Addie and the chili. The incident involved some bowls of chili, and more than one woman crying, in fact several women crying, and also had something to do with our country's political mistakes, and the mistakes we ourselves make with our children. "Addie and the Chili," I was going to call it, because sitting in the middle of the scene were three bowls of chili on the restaurant table, or rather two bowls and one cup, the cup being mine.

I made an attempt at writing the story and then gave up. I don't know whether the story defeated me or I simply became distracted by other things. I was a single mother at the time, and trying to support myself and my child. I was trying to write stories at the same time as I was working and caring for my child, and I often did not finish what I started. Now, more than thirty years have gone by, and I'll give it another try.

I ordered only a cup of chili, not a bowl, because I was upset and thought I would not be able to eat more. I was upset by the movie and by Addie. Addie ordered a bowl when she was still in a good mood, talking her head off, before she knew what I was going to say to her, and then, after I said it, when the waiter set the bowl down in front of her, she could not eat any of the chili, or at least she said she could not. As for Ellie, she ordered a bowl because she was very hungry, despite being, like me, upset by the movie and by Addie. She finished her bowl quickly, though I didn't notice her eating. Maybe she was eating her chili while I was reproaching and insulting Addie and Addie was reacting—too hungry to wait. Ellie then sat there, still hungry, staring at Addie's untouched bowl. She told me later that she had wanted to ask Addie for it, but did not, because she knew how offensive it would be to ask a woman in tears for her chili.

What started the trouble was the movie Ellie and I saw earlier in the evening. It was a recently released movie about some devastating things that had happened in another part of the world that caused a great many children to suffer. Or rather, everyone suffered, old and young, but the movie showed the children especially, and it is always hard to accept the idea of children suffering at all.

Things had also been happening in Ellie's life and in my life that made us more vulnerable than usual to such a film, although I can't remember now what those things were, and we came out of it exhausted by the sustained grief of the story. Others in the audience were clearly just as upset. Two men were evidently not able to leave the theater at all, and sat there side by side staring straight ahead at the empty screen. Women I saw in the line to use the ladies' room had been crying or were still crying, or trying not to cry.

Then we walked from the movie theater to pick up Addie where she was living nearby, in a brownstone, and as soon as she came down the front stoop she began talking about herself. Addie always talked mainly about herself, and she probably still does—I don't know her anymore, though not because of that evening. I try to think why Ellie and I remained friends with her. It must be that at times she did talk about other things, and said intelligent things about subjects that Ellie and I were both interested in.

As she began talking about herself, on this night, she further upset me by addressing her remarks exclusively to Ellie, at least in the beginning. As I listened, I became very angry, though I kept quiet. I was angry at Addie for what she was saying, the way she was saying it, and what that told me about her life and her character, but there was more going on, there were other things feeding into my anger at Addie.

I was angry at everything that had happened in the film, everything that had happened that day to me, and that week to me, and several things concerning my child, and several things concerning two friends who had attempted to commit suicide just the week before and which I had heard about, in one case directly from the friend herself—how she had managed to call 911 and had been carried from her apartment on a stretcher. It had not been a good couple of weeks, there in the dead of winter, and my anger at all of it boiled up in me when Addie began telling us something involving a lover, a story she clearly believed to be tragic and exciting, with herself at center stage, but that was, to me, and probably to Ellie, only dull and sordid.

It is possible that on another evening, after a different couple of weeks and a different film, or even at a different time of year, in midsummer out on the sidewalk, with a warm breeze blowing, I might have been interested in this story about an angry lover, phone calls at three and four in the morning, the offering of a bouquet of flowers, the bouquet torn from the vase and thrown in her face, the demand for the repayment of fifty dollars, the subsequent humiliation on the lover's part, his begging for forgiveness, and probably the forgiveness withheld. (I remember everything but that last—whether Addie forgave him.) One of the things we must have enjoyed about Addie, in fact, was her often absurd tales of love affairs. I remember only one longtime lover, or perhaps even husband, who used to cradle her feet in his lap and groom them, which I thought rather touching and which did not fit with what was otherwise the style of her love life.

But on this evening, as we walked toward the restaurant, with a bitter wind blowing and slush at the curb, I was ready to give up on our plan to have dinner. I was ready to leave for home, though my small apartment would hardly have been inviting, and would feel particularly empty since I had not planned to be there at that hour. I said I was tired and going home, but I was persuaded to stay, not only by Ellie, because she did not want to be alone with Addie, I'm sure, but also by Addie, no doubt because she wanted more of an audience than Ellie.

We went into the restaurant and sat down. As I began to read the menu, while Addie continued talking, I discovered that I was crying and did not want to eat or drink or talk. I made up my mind, then, to speak frankly, because I could not pretend that nothing was wrong.

I then turned to Addie and told her that there was something I wanted to say. She looked me in the eye, and her expression was fiercer than I had expected, as though she knew in advance that something unpleasant was coming and had resolved not to listen to me. Before I could go on, however, the waiter came up to our table, a tall young man with chubby arms, and said, "What can I do for you ladies?" That was when we ordered the chili, and the waiter did not seem very pleased.

When he left, Addie looked at me again, and I went ahead, though I did not think that what I said would have much of an effect. I said I was offended by her, I was offended by the way she came out of her house and did not first ask us how we were and how the movie was, or even look carefully at us or think of us before she began to talk about herself and tell us her story. I said that she should try to read our mood and be sensitive to us, that she was so wrapped up in herself she hardly saw us, that she did not seem to care about us but only saw us as an audience for her.

Right away she said she could not hear any more and began to cry. Then I saw that by her reaction she had made me look mean and that she had also held on to center stage, remained the star, though now in a different drama. Now

I was yet another of the people who had wronged and hurt her. She said she was going to leave and took out money to pay for the chili. I don't know what I had imagined her reaction would be—contrition, shame, apology?

Ellie began trying to make peace between us. I, too, thought I would have to keep her there and let her tell her story sooner or later, or the evening would be spoiled anyway. I'm not sure that I would, now, feel the same way I did then, so it is hard for me to understand my reaction then. Now I would probably have let her go, and written her off, and spent the rest of the evening talking with Ellie. But in any case, I did what I could to mollify her, though I was annoyed doing it. I did what I could to get her back to her story and draw her out. It was not working.

I did feel better now, though, having said what was on my mind, and I ate my cup of chili easily and was sorry I had not ordered a bowl. Then, because I was tired of trying to persuade Addie to talk, I turned to Ellie. We talked about trips we were both going to be taking soon, and then jobs that Ellie was having trouble getting, and then a certain man's opinion of her that she was worried about—she said that when she had nothing else to worry about, she worried about what this man thought of her.

Meanwhile, Addie sat with her head bowed, dabbing at the surface of her chili with her spoon and sniffing. So then I turned to Addie again, and persuaded her to tell us what had been happening that day with her lover, and she began to talk again. She talked about not only this lover, but about a gourmet cook she had picked up on the street and who had come to see her that morning between eight and nine o'clock. She talked then about another man, a busy screenplay writer who wrote her long letters even though he lived right here in the city. During this, Ellie did not say a word. She had finished her chili. Maybe she was cross because she had not asked Addie for her chili and she was still hungry. She kept looking at Addie's chili. But I think she was also becoming truly angry herself now, because Addie was doing just what she had wanted to do in the beginning and what was really so offensive to both of us—talking her head off to a captive audience about the men who loved her.

I will ask Ellie if there is more that she remembers, but after all, I see why the story was difficult to write—most of all because, as is true of many stories in real life, not much had happened. All that had happened was that certain emotions had shifted around from person to person over that hour or so. Addie started out cheerful, became angry and hurt, and then recovered her good cheer. I started out upset by the movie, became more upset and angry, and then felt better once I had spoken my mind to Addie, though subsequently annoyed by her manipulation. Ellie started out upset by the movie, became angry at Addie, though not as angry as I was, recovered her equanimity in attempting to act as mediator in the conflict between me and Addie, and then, in turn, once Addie recovered her good spirits and I attempted to placate her, became even angrier at Addie.

But it is interesting, in its own way, to think what happens after a movie is made and people see the movie. A movie is made depicting how badly people are hurt in a war, and it is skillfully made, so that it affects the people who see it. They cry or nearly cry, or simply feel their grief and shame without showing it. And when the movie is over, they disperse, they go off in different directions. And some of them may have trouble eating, then, and also vent their emotions on their friends, whose failings seem less forgivable after what was depicted in the movie.

Now I've asked Ellie, but she has forgotten the evening entirely, and certainly does not remember asking me to write about it. It is strange that I was so sure she would never forget it. But, prompted by my question, she thought hard and remembered Addie's full name, and then looked her up, which I had not done, and located her, now living in Europe. For me, Addie had dropped out of existence once I no longer knew her. Ellie discovered that Addie has even done some rather interesting things. Our lives go on, years pass, we start things and finish them, year by year, things add up to our credit. Maybe that is why we were friends with her for as long as we were—not only because she and her stories amused us, but also because she had some interesting ambitions, and was not unintelligent, besides also being so silly and self-absorbed. Though all three of us could be that, she was the silliest of us.

As for what happened to Addie's chili, that evening, she asked the waiter if he could wrap it up for her so that she could take it home. We did not much like the waiter, in part because he clearly did not much like us—these three women arguing and crying, who had ordered nothing more than some chili. He said the restaurant had no containers for that, "as such," but that he would wrap it up for her the way it was, in the bowl, and ask her to bring the bowl back. She lived nearby, she could return the bowl the next day, and that is what Addie did, as far as I know.

Tantrums

She is feeling out of control and uncomfortable in her body (she is pregnant). He becomes annoyed: "You're always calling attention to yourself. I have a very tough weekend ahead of me." She agrees, but it is hard, when she feels this way. She would like to just give up and go to bed, but she can't. She has to go on trying to make dinner. But as she lifts four pieces of chicken on one sheet of tinfoil, a piece drops to the floor. "Damn you!" she cries out to the chicken. Much later, when they are about to go to bed, yet another call comes from his brother, who is mentally ill. This brother has strange ideas about what they should all do together and also about carrying things: he thinks that everyone must carry a mental potato with which to get on in life, and sometimes thinks he is a turtle carrying a loaf of bread under his arm. As often before, she has taken the call, to protect her husband. This time, after she talks to him, she really begins bawling and pounds her fists on the walls. She can't stand his invasion into their life. She is furious, even though at other times she has been full of compassion. She knows the man is not responsible for what he says.

Claim to Fame #7: A. J. Ayer

The older half-sister of an early boyfriend of mine, it was revealed many decades after her conception, was the daughter, until then unacknowledged, of the British philosopher and Oxford don A. J. Ayer. (Upon his death what he left her was the choice, out of his library, of a single book.)

Young Housewife

That day, how she saw herself:
stocky in shorts,
limp hair, bristling legs,
trudging out into the yard with the baby
and then later into the yard again
with the laundry.
But wasn't it also the truth now?

Here in the Country

Here in the country there are yards full of rusting cars, kept for spare parts. A pale little girl sticks her fingers in her ears at the roar of a family engine.

The same people appear at every store because here they all do their shopping on the same afternoon at the same stores.

A raffle prize is a chain saw, and this already seems desirable to us.

All the neighbors have too much lettuce to use, in their gardens—and so do we.

Birds nest under the air conditioner and on the back porch inside a bamboo shade that we rolled up early in the spring to let more light into the bathroom.

Bats spend a few days, maybe longer, behind the chimney. In the evening we see them fly out, one by one, at short intervals, five or six of them, like carrier pigeons starting off on a race. They dive in the air and fly low over the lawn. Later they squeak by an upstairs window and scratch the wooden clapboards going in and out of the attic.

Hornets have built a conical nest under the front porch eave. One evening at dusk, we knock it down. It is in layers like fine pastry.

There are tidy little homes with thriving gardens and lawns perfectly smooth, dark green and unblemished. Stiff, short evergreen shrubs hug this tidy house, and one brown goose walks down the driveway followed by two white geese. But the people who come out of the house have a scowling, proprietary air, as stout and scruffy as old dogs.

Sheets of plastic cover the windows of other houses, and the back porches are crowded with junk.

Bees live in a hollow tree at the end of the driveway, behind a black-painted sheet of metal that was nailed over the hole long ago. In hot weather, more and more of them cling to the trunk by their hive, walking over one another until they have formed a thick golden beard on the tree.

When the cooler weather comes again, the beard is gone.

A black butterfly fans its wings slowly to dry them, riding on a leaf of pachysandra. Powder-blue spots line the lower edges of its wings, and the undersides, like a peacock's tail, have iridescent eyes.

At the back of our backyard we hear the screams of the neighbor children and the clear, logical shouts of the mother: "I'm giving you fair warning: Get off my back!"

On some days, mysterious vibrations shake the house as though some enormous person were throwing himself against the front door.

On the way to the general store we pass an overgrown lot with four tall poles forming a rectangle. Parked in the rectangle is a small, unused trailer.

The neighbors' two dogs bark and bark. They may be barking at each other, but they may be barking together at some third thing.

The hardworking old man two houses away from us cannot be idle. If he is not tending someone else's property, he rakes his own gravel, or weeds his own vegetable garden. We hear the metal wheelbarrow rattling over his lawn. Sometimes he comes to the house next door to feed the cats on the side porch: "C'mon, kitty kitty," he calls gently. "C'mon, kitty kitty. You hungry? You hungry?"

Egg

The word for egg in Dutch is *ei*. In German it is *Ei*, in Yiddish *ey*, in Old English *ey*. The word for egg in Norwegian is *egg*, in Icelandic it is *egg*, in Faroese *egg*, in Swedish *ägg*, in Danish *æg*. In Old Norse the word is *egg*, in Middle English *egge*. (In French it is *oeuf*.) (In Scots Gaelic it is *ugh*.)

Two American babies, long ago, are learning to speak—they are learning English, they have no choice. They are close to eighteen months old, one is a week older than the other. Sometimes they fight over a toy, at other times they play quietly by themselves in the same room.

On the living room floor, today, one baby sees a round white thing on the rug. He gets to his feet, with some difficulty, and toddles over to it. He says "Eck?" At this, the other one looks up, interested, gets to his feet, also with some difficulty, toddles over to see, and says "Ack!" They're learning the word, they've almost got it. It does not matter that the round white object is not an egg but a ping-pong ball. In time, they will learn this, too.

The Afternoon of a Translator

Although she is late, she has stopped, before coming up out of the subway, to look at herself in the mirror of the subway toilet. She had thought she was well dressed when she left home, but decides that she is not. She is carrying a folder of work and two books. She walks west from the subway toward the home of the wealthy anthropologist who may have work for her. She is thinking nervously of other things and does not look where she is walking. She steps in a large soft turd that a dog has deposited on the sidewalk. As she tries to remove what is on her shoe, a young man who appears to be simpleminded stops to offer advice, then stays to watch with friendly interest as she scrapes her foot on the curb.

When she arrives at the pretty town house, she rings the doorbell down in the areaway below ground level. The German housekeeper who answers the door has been ironing shirts in the kitchen. The man who lives alone here comes running down the stairs to shake her hand. He has dark eyes and locks of loose dark hair that fall over his forehead as he talks. He is wearing a white shirt and black pants.

The phone rings almost immediately, and as he answers it and speaks in Italian, she goes into the nearby bathroom to wash her hands and inspect her shoe. On the wall next to her hangs a small painting of a piece of bread.

When she comes out, he is still talking, and she crosses the room to look through the plate glass wall at the bare garden. When he is finished talking, he leads her upstairs to a hall filled with African sculptures. As they then climb higher up in the house, passing other rooms, she sees in one of the bedrooms a child's crib. He later tells her he has a two-year-old son who lives in Mexico.

At the top of the house, the walls of the man's study are lined with white-jacketed books, so clean they look as if they have never been opened. She spends a cordial hour with him discussing a piece of translation work that he would like her to do, as well as, more generally, languages, writing, life in the city, and life in the country.

She leaves feeling stimulated by the visit and the prospect of work, and goes to a nearby department store to shop. She stays there for three hours, but buys only a single pair of red shorts for eleven dollars, before going back down into the subway to return home.

At the Movies Last Night

At the movies last night,
we saw,
along with two van-loads of inmates
from the Wingdale Psychiatric Center:
The Seven-Per-Cent Solution.

Sunday Night at the Summer Cottages

It is Sunday night and some weekend guests who have been visiting the people in the little cottages by the lake are leaving now for the city in the dark, and a few people, the people who stay in the cottages all summer, are walking them down to their cars. They aren't many but they have all come down at the same time and in this still, silent place it makes for some confusion. Leah the vegetarian from deep inside her neck brace says, Look at this, Look how many people. And little enough happens here so that this has an air of something happening. Flashlights from out of the dark beam over the ground, the boulders shining in the road, and the many moving legs, but the faces are hidden. Leah's white bra straps escape her dress and fall over her thick arms. She is a small woman full of warnings, about the stones and roots in the path, and her husband Henry chides her gently.

A Theory

Off the shores of our land are clods of earth like stepping stones in great numbers. From each clod rises a thin metal pole. Between the poles stretch loosely hung wires connecting each pole to more than one other, so that there is a great web of silver wires in the air about fifteen feet above the water. We are not sure what purpose the structure served in earlier times. It might have been a way of generating electricity. Perhaps a bolt of lightning struck one pole, at random, then traveled through the wires, which are haphazardly interconnected. In its search for an outlet, it increased in velocity so much that when an outlet was finally provided, the electricity was powerful enough to light several houses. This is my theory—though I have never actually seen the outlet. Then again, there are rarely any thunderstorms here, when I come to think of it, perhaps seven or eight every August and one in July.

II

Community Notice:
Example of Redundancy

This is a reminder
that today
the community
will be gathering
this afternoon
to come together
as a community.

Conversation at Noisy Party on Snowy Winter Afternoon in Country

Airline pilot:

–I found a very small owl by the road, this big. *(He holds his hands eight inches apart.)* It was very beautiful, perfect.

Birder is quick to respond:

–So what.

Pilot is puzzled. He thought she would be interested.

–So what? he says.

Birder laughs. Others are there, listening. They laugh.

–No, I said *saw whet*. I'd have to look in the book, but I think that's what it is.

He is still puzzled.

–A what?

–A saw whet. S-a-w. W-h-e-t.

–Oh! Well. *(Pause.)* I thought it might be a screech owl.

–It might be. I'll have to look.

–They're small too, aren't they?

—Yes, they're very small. But they make a very loud noise.

—It has no blood on it. I think it must have been hit by a car. *(The others nod.)* It must have broken its neck. *(The others nod again.)* I can give it to you if you want.

—Sure, I'll put it in my freezer.

He laughs. They laugh.

Birder goes on:

—I once had a weasel in my freezer.

He laughs again. They all laugh again.

—It was in my freezer for two years.

They laugh again.

—I was waiting for John Berry to come pick it up.

One woman asks:

—Is he a taxidermist?

—No, he's just interested in weasels. *(They wait to hear more.)* It was a small weasel. It was the only thing in my freezer. Besides the vodka.

They laugh again. Another woman adds:

—Well, as long as you could still get to the vodka . . .

A Question for the Writing Class Concerning a Type of Furniture

Can you create
a tragic scene
in which you mention
the bibelots and whimsies
on the whatnot?

In a Hotel Room in Ithaca

April, the housekeeper,
has left a message for me
hand-written in red ink on a piece of paper.
It is lying next to the coffee maker.
She has written: "Wisdom begins in wonder."
The quotation is from Socrates.
But the smiley face has been added by April.

Incident on the Train

I'm on the train, traveling alone, with two seats to myself. I have to use the restroom. Without thinking about it carefully, I ask a couple across the aisle if they would please watch my things for me for a moment. Then I take a closer look at them and have second thoughts: they are young, for one thing. Also, they seem very nervous, the guy's eyes are bloodshot, and the girl has a lot of tattoos. Still, it's done now. I get up and start moving back. But, as a precaution, I ask someone, a man a few seats behind me, who is dressed in a suit and looks like a businessman, to please keep an eye on that young couple for me, because I have had to leave my seat for a moment and all my things are on it. I could just go back and retrieve my bag, giving an excuse—in fact, this is suggested by the man, who objects to being put in that position, the position of having to stop what he is doing and watch a young couple who have done nothing wrong—so far anyway. But I feel it is too awkward to go and get my bag, and even if I went and got my bag, I would still be leaving on my seat a valuable coat.

—Can't you wait? asks the man, though it's none of his business.

—No. Then I have another idea: Maybe you could go sit in my seat while I'm gone?

—No, says the man—then I'd have to leave *my* things.

He is not being very cooperative. I say, But that lady across the aisle could watch them for you—she looks trustworthy. She's old and she's sitting very still.

—She's asleep.

—You could wake her up.

—I wouldn't want to do that.

The old lady is sitting next to a younger woman. The younger woman is slumped over, asleep, and the old lady is also slumped over, leaning against her.

—Just nudge her a little.

—No, I won't. In fact, I don't think she's asleep—she may be dead.

I think he's joking, though I'm not sure.

Our voices have been rising. Now the people around us are disturbed by our conversation and by me standing over him in the aisle. All except for the old lady, who really might be dead. Her mouth is open but I can't see if her eyes are open.

—Can you keep it down? someone says. It's the woman on the far side of the old lady. She has woken up and is glaring at us. My mom is sleeping, she says.

I don't like her tone. Now I get a little aggressive.

—I thought she was dead, I say.

The woman elbows the old lady, and says, Mom, tell this goofball you're not dead.

The old lady opens her eyes and looks blankly at her daughter. I'm not your mother, she says.

—Oh brother, says the daughter.

Meanwhile, someone behind them is beginning to hum. It's a teenage girl, or maybe she's a little younger, maybe twelve. The humming is getting to me, given all the commotion that is already going on. I'm sensitive to noise.

—Why is she humming? I ask the woman next to her, who seems to be her mother.

Her mother says, It's you guys—you're making her nervous, she hums when she's nervous or people talk too much, when anyone talks too much.

She stares at us, though peacefully, while the girl continues humming. Now I am interested. Some other people have turned around to look at her. The old lady tries to turn her head, but she can't turn it very far.

The girl's mother continues to explain her daughter's neurosis. The girl is humming louder.

The old lady is becoming agitated. She looks at each person around her and then glares at the woman next to her, saying, I don't know you from Adam!

I still have to go to the bathroom, though I forgot it for a while.

Now the businessman, having lost patience, gets up and says, All right, I'll go sit in your seat. Just get going and come back. Let's get this brouhaha over with.

I think that's a strange choice of word, especially for a businessman, but I don't say so.

He pushes past me and goes to my seat. I want to make sure he sits in the right place. I have taken two seats, as I said, and they're on the side by the river. He bends over, moves my coat, and sits down in the aisle seat. Now, through the noise of the old lady and the girl behind her, who is still humming, though her mother has stopped talking, I hear the young man with the bloodshot eyes saying loudly, Hey man, there's someone sitting there.

The businessman says he knows, and that she asked him to hold her seat.

The young man is surprised. Why would she do that? he asks. The businessman is silent, probably thinking what he should say.

The young man waits. Then he says, Really?

—She asked me to sit here while she was in the restroom, says the businessman.

—Why, man? That doesn't make sense, says the young man. He seems a little defensive.

The businessman is still silent. Finally he just shrugs.

—Oh, for Christ's sake, says the young man, for Christ's sake. Goddamn.

But he says it quietly. He is still saying it when I walk away up the aisle. And I'm feeling a little bad about making such a fuss, since, after all, he is trying to defend my seat, so maybe I was wrong about him in the first place, him and his tattooed girlfriend. I didn't trust them, just because they were young. On the other hand, his language was pretty bad.

Letter to the Father

Celan, talking about Kafka, says: "A poem is always a letter to the father."

I tell this to my friend the poet.

My friend the poet responds:

"Celan must have had a different father than I did."

He stops to think and then asks, "Than I do? . . ."

His father is dead.

"Do I have a father, or did I have a father?"

I can't answer that question.

Conversation at Noisy Party on Snowy Winter Afternoon in Country (Short Version)

Airline pilot: I found a little owl by the side of the road, about this big. *(Holds hands about eight inches apart.)*

Birder: Say what?

Pilot: I said I found a little owl, a very beautiful thing, dead by the side of the road.

Birder: Saw *what*?

Pilot: A little owl, it had no blood on it. It was perfect. I think it was hit by a car.

Birder: So what!

Pilot: *(Pause)* Well, I thought you'd be interested . . .

Birder: Saw whet!

Pilot: What?

Birder: *Saw whet!*

Democracy in France, in 1884

Henry James, in *A Little Tour*, describes what he calls democracy as it prevails in France: A waiter brings a customer, in a cafe, some writing materials. Then, the cafe being quiet, and the waiter having nothing else to do, he sits down with the customer at the table and proceeds to write a letter himself.

Claim to Fame #8: On the Way to Detroit

In the airplane on my way to Detroit, on a recent trip, I sat next to a woman who turned out to be the widow of the nephew of Lewis Mumford!

England

My left hand keeps trying to type another *e* into the word *acknowledgment*, making it *acknowledgement*—the British spelling—while my right hand keeps deleting the *e*. Maybe my left hand grew up in England.

Criminal Activity in Historic Colonial Williamsburg

During a block party, a tourist enters a gift shop holding an open container of beer. She is a little tipsy, a little loud, and talkative, and won't leave, though she stays near the door. The shop owner is annoyed and asks her several times to leave. The woman persists in staying where she is. A shop employee is watching from the back. After some discussion, the shop owner calls the police, and the woman is arrested for being drunk and disorderly. Months later, the case goes to court. A witness is called for the defense: it is the gift shop employee, who is sympathetic to the accused. The woman with the open container was doing no harm, she says, she was not really drunk or disorderly. There is no witness for the prosecution. The judge, exasperated, dismisses the case.

Conversation in Hotel Lounge

Two women sit together on the sofa in the hotel lounge, bent over and deep in conversation. I am walking through, on the way to my room.

First woman, loudly and distinctly, happily: "I never had *fun* before!"

I am surprised and intrigued—what a heart-to-heart they are having! I try to imagine her life up to now. I try to imagine what she has been experiencing recently, and also the revelation this must be to her—the concept of *fun*. My thoughts take just a moment.

Second woman, speaking softly, inaudibly: "[Mumble, mumble]."

First woman: "No, no. *Fun* is a Chinese word. *Fun* is Mandarin. It means . . . a kind of rice noodle!"

Claim to Fame #9: In Detroit

In Detroit, standing in a line, I met a woman who turned out to be the daughter of Samuel Beckett's publisher Barney Rossett.

A Friend Borrows a Better Shopping Cart

A man who collects old televisions, old telephones, old magazines, and other old things says to his friend, “Oh no, don’t throw them out!” He’s talking about a pair of very large and very old speakers. He says he will take them. He travels by subway from another part of the city, bringing with him his shopping cart. The speakers are so large that only one will fit in the shopping cart. He takes it by subway back to his apartment. He returns for the other speaker, but this time without his shopping cart. He has noticed that his friend has a better shopping cart, so he borrows that one. Does he return it right away? Yes, he returns it right away, again coming by subway. Why didn’t he take both speakers at once, in a cab? Well, that might have worked, they might have fit next to him on the back seat, and he can afford a long cab ride. But he won’t spend any more than he has to. Among his group of friends, he has the most money and is also the only *tightwad*.

Sabbath Story #1: Circuit Breaker

Heat wave in city.

Orthodox Jew stands on sidewalk waiting for non-Jew to come along.

Non-Jew, stranger, comes along.

Will stranger help Jew?

Jew takes stranger into building and down into basement.

Stranger flips circuit breaker switch.

Now air-conditioning unit comes on again.

Upstairs in apartment, many men are sitting in undershirts sweating in heat.

Stranger is offered milk and cookies, in thanks.

Letter to the U.S. Postal Service Concerning a Poster

Dear Postal Service,

I was in my local post office the other day, and while I waited in line I had time to examine a poster that was displayed there. It was large (about three feet by four feet) and brightly colored, and it said, in very large letters, "People are good." The picture behind the words showed the inside of a very large cardboard carton with a few Styrofoam peanuts in the bottom. The text of the poster concerned sending a pair of shoes packed in a large box full of Styrofoam peanuts. I expected the message to be environmental, asking us to consider the waste involved before we overpackaged what we were sending.

I have often been annoyed by receiving items unnecessarily packed in Styrofoam peanuts. I try to collect the peanuts and put them into a plastic bag to take to my local packing and mailing service for reuse, since I don't like to throw something into the landfill that will never break down, and I am then further annoyed. With what I imagine must be static electricity, the peanuts cling to my hands, my hair, and everything else nearby, so that they are difficult to pick up and even more difficult, since they weigh almost nothing, to shake into the bag.

I always enjoy reading posters that agree with a favorite position of my own. But as I read further I was shocked to discover the message this poster, co-sponsored by an internet auction service, was conveying: that sending a pair of shoes packed in an outsized box filled with Styrofoam peanuts was what you or your writers or their writers called "a kind of love."

This seems wrong to me for several reasons. As I understand it, people shipping items that have been purchased through an internet auction are strangers to the people buying these items, and the transaction is purely commercial. If they pack the purchased item with great care, it is either because they are conscientious or because they want to ensure that their ratings remain high and they will be able to sell more items in the future. It is not out of any sort of love, which they could not feel for a stranger unless they were truly enlightened, which most people are not. But worse than that misconception is the larger message: that overpackaging is good, or at least merely a harmless, rather charming foible. To send an item like an unbreakable pair of shoes in such excessive packaging demonstrates no love for the environment, and without love for the environment any other form of love is less admirable, in my opinion, though that is just an opinion. You are surely only encouraging the sort of wastefulness of which our society is already sufficiently guilty. As a government agency, you ought to be particularly concerned about this.

Please reconsider the message you want to send.

Yours sincerely.

Mature Woman Toward the End of a Discussion About Raincoats over Lunch with Another Mature Woman

She says, in a reasonable tone,
"It doesn't *have* to be a Burberry!"

Sabbath Story #2: Minyan

Man is standing on sidewalk outside synagogue holding cell phone.

Stranger comes along and asks man if he can use cell phone.

Man agrees, stranger makes call.

Man then asks in turn if stranger will come inside synagogue.

Needed: one more man to make up minyan.

Stranger agrees, stays for most of service.

Our Network

The more time goes by, the more people we attach to ourselves. I do not hire a lawyer except in special circumstances, when I want to threaten my relatives or my former husband or my landlady. But I do have a therapist, a stockbroker, and an accountant who I see regularly. And it is of course quite likely that my stockbroker has a therapist, and that his therapist has a lawyer. No doubt that lawyer also has a therapist, an accountant, and possibly his own lawyer. This association of professional people providing essential services is a very strong network in our community.

William Cobbett and the Stranger

A man, a stranger to him, asked Cobbett why he looked so fresh and young. Cobbett said he rose early, went to bed early, ate sparingly, never drank anything stronger than small beer, shaved once a day, and washed his hands and face clean three times a day at the very least.

The stranger responded that that was too much to think of doing.

Claim to Fame #3: June Havoc

My parents bought a small house in Connecticut from June Havoc, a talented actress and tap dancer even as a tiny child. She was not as well known, however, as her sister, Gypsy Rose Lee.

A Matter of Perspective

I saw something white moving through the air by the side of
the house.
I thought it was a large white butterfly fluttering by—
a rare white butterfly!
But it was only a special delivery letter,
coming past the window in the postman's hand.

Master Builder

With most excellent workmanship
he is up there on his ladder,
with greatest care ruining
the oldest house in town.

Enemies

Enemies : One way to say it

I have an enemy, I never had an enemy before.

Actually, now I have two enemies. No, I have only one, still; but he now has one, and because he is my partner, his enemy must become my enemy. And because his enemy's partner is supporting the case of his enemy, his enemy's partner must become my enemy, too.

Enemies : Another way to say it

We have some enemies, now. We never had enemies before. Or at least I never did. He did. Now together we have at least two. He had some, down in the city and also near here. Now we have one who is really only mine, unless she includes him in her anger. And we have another, or two, if the woman is going to join the man in turning against us. We don't know that yet. They, or he, really started out as his enemies, or enemy, but if I am going to take his side, they will have to become my enemies too. These enemies are both, or all, here in town, or near enough. It will be awkward and unpleasant, or sad, to meet them on the street. I have never been in that position before, of finding it embarrassing to meet someone on the street, an enemy.

Lonely (Canned Ham)

The thin little old woman
goes timidly
into a shop
on the day before Thanksgiving.
She asks:
"Do you have a canned ham?"

That Obnoxious Man

That obnoxious man! I saw him on the train the other day and I knew who he was, but I couldn't remember his name. I kept thinking about him after that, trying to remember his name. He was so obnoxious, long ago, when I knew him. By now his hair is white, but he still has that way of staring straight at you like a frightened rabbit with his eyes bugging out.

I am on the train again today, and I wish he would get on. Then I would ask him what his name was. Maybe after that I could stop thinking about him.

The beginning of this—"That obnoxious man!"—made me think of a poem by Lorine Niedecker. Or else it is the other way around, and it is because of the Lorine Niedecker poem that I say "That obnoxious man!" Her poem goes:

(untitled)

The museum man!
I wish he'd taken Pa's spitbox!
I'm going to take that spitbox out
and bury it in the ground
and put a stone on top.
Because without that stone on top
it would come back.

Actually, it probably worked both ways: I began the story with those words because somewhere in my memory, though I didn't know it, was the Niedecker poem. Then, when I looked at my story, it reminded me of the poem.

Now I might write it in a different way, more like her poem:

That obnoxious man!
I saw him on the train and I knew exactly who he was,
from long ago!
But I couldn't remember his name.
Oh, I wish he'd get on the train again
so I could ask him his name.
Then I could bury him
And put a stone on top.

Wistful Spinster

What is that,
touching her so lightly in the bath
as she lies back in the warm water?
Ah,
a floating bookmark . . .

Old Men Around Town

In our town an old man used to come out of his house and take his daily walk along the sides of the streets. There were not many sidewalks, so he shared the street with the cars, but in the back streets the cars went by slowly. He was a tall, thin old man with a slight stoop—the father of the doctor in our town. He held his cane in one hand and a cloth bag in the other, for the mail, and he walked briskly but with such small steps that he did not advance very fast.

He seems to be gone now. The warm weather has returned, but he does not appear on the streets. In the cold weather there are no old men on the streets. Now that the warm weather has come, a few old men have appeared, but we see them only in the center of the town, walking a short distance along a sidewalk to enter a shop or standing at a street crossing. One of them is fleshy and bearded, in shorts and suspenders, dark socks and sturdy shoes. Another is bone thin and totters, swaying to one side, resting a hand against whatever bit of wall is nearby, or leaning far back to open a shop door.

Another old man used to walk past our house. He had good balance and a longer step. He wore a tam-o'-shanter at an angle on his handsome head. His white beard was short and curly. He had lived in the town all his life, unlike the doctor's father, and he would stop to tell us where the sidewalks used to be and who had died a violent death, in which house. We no longer see him these days.

Yet another old man, once a week, would stand dressed in a suit and overcoat by his gate, in polished formal shoes. He was out early, waiting to be picked up by his son.

We see these old men on the streets of our town, and we see others in a nursing home, where they have been left by their families. The nursing home is itself like a little town, with its own chapel, barbershop, gift shop, and community meeting room like a town hall. There are the offices of the administrators, and there is the hallway like Main Street. There you may meet the others from the town and stop to talk with them. Some of the residents, though, spend the whole day going up and down the hall. They have given up stopping to chat, if they ever did, and as they pass you, they stare hard at you, almost with hostility, or else look straight ahead with vacant eyes.

One of them, fine-featured, neatly dressed, who walks briskly, with a vigorous step, mutters to himself about his men and what work they will be doing today. He stops to tell us that he must be up early in the morning—to get down to the factory. The factory is gone, his men are gone, but he still seems to be in charge of something.

A large-framed, tall, and bony old man still has all his wits about him. He sits in his wheelchair in the doorway to his room, facing out into the hall, and if we stop to talk to him, he tells us about his life as a wool sorter and grader in Australia. His wife visits him almost every day and spends many hours there, sitting in a chair next to him, their little dog on his lap brightly observing the foot traffic and wheelchair traffic as it goes by.

Lying in his white-sheeted bed is another old man, the professor, with skin almost as white as his sheets. In a nearby bed lies his roommate, his skin dark brown. They are good friends and are affectionate with each other, though the roommate has more of his wits about him than the professor. The roommate enjoys his visits from his family, but does not like to leave his room. The old professor has lost a lot of his memory, though not his sense of humor. He tries to make a joke, but he does not speak clearly, and only his family can guess what he is saying. He knows who his visitors are, but he does not remember what he has done in his life. His family wheel him out of his room in his wheelchair and down the hall. At mealtimes, they take him to the dining room, where they help him to eat his food.

In a village we have been reading about, two hundred years ago, an old man would live out his days, whatever his condition, either in his own home or in the home of a relative or perhaps another person paid to look after him. He might be a burden to his family, or he might find small ways to help them. As long as he could get about under his own power, he might roam the streets or the fields, the meadows or the woods. Then one day he would be struck down by illness or accident, and die slowly or quickly.

Amiel Weekes, elderly though not yet near the end of his life, lived by himself on the south side of the village overlooking the sea and the woods. Every Saturday afternoon, when the sun was still high, he would come in from his work, wash, shave, and eat his frugal supper of bread and milk. Then he would sit down to read his Bible. In this way, he began his Sabbath.

Old Uncle Jonathan came to mortise posts and set fence. The children thought no other man in the town could mortise posts. Then, when the sun approached the Northern Tropic, he would come again with his hoe to plant corn, and he would come again when the corn was up. The children would gather around Uncle Jonathan, for he had a kind gaze and a kind voice for children, and they liked to look on, hour after hour, when he mortised posts or spliced rails.

He was tall and athletic, and limped from rheumatism. He would stop work to take some refreshment regularly at eleven and again at four o'clock, when he would lay down his tools and have a little rum, salt-fish, and crackers. His face was dignified, with a high intellectual forehead, and his mind was probably equally intellectual, but he was modest in expressing his thoughts. Like others of that time, he lived in obscurity, poor, working for his daily bread, at last dying of old age, mourned for only a few days and forgotten.

Ebenezer Brooks, another old man in the same village, had prominent eyes, a large Roman nose, and a broad, sloping forehead. His hair was silvery white, and hung down on either side of his spectacles as he sat leaning back in his chair by the side of the fireplace, reading the great Bible or sleeping over it in his quiet home.

Old Uncle Eben was Ebenezer's son. In late middle age, a stroke deprived him of the use of one half of his body and he became a heavy burden to his family. For ten years he sat in his chair or moved about by leaning on the top of it, shifting it forward, and leaning again on the top of it. He spoke in monosyllables but never clearly enough to be understood. He would take up a pencil in his left hand and scratch a few words with it.

He used to hobble over to his brother Obed's house, leaning on his chair back and hauling it along, resting often in the chair when he grew tired. He returned less and less often to his own house. At last he remained in Obed's house, sitting by the kitchen window or on a plot of grass in warm weather or standing in the woodshed in winter. There, for many years, with his left hand, he would saw and split kindling. At last he contracted an inflammation of the bowels and died.

And then there was George Weekes, who would wander from place to place, restlessly, all day long, returning to the home of the relative who looked after him only at nightfall or when he was hungry or tired. One winter day, he had traveled farther from home than usual. It began to snow and the east wind was blowing. The snowflakes fell on him more and more thickly. The storm and darkness gathered upon him when he was still far away from the fireside and evening meal that was waiting for him. The nor'easter howled through the trees and the snow encased their trunks and loaded down their branches and filled up all the sheltered spots in the landscape. Old George retraced his steps to the nearest house, but the only ones at home were children, and they were afraid to let him in. So he returned to the valley that he had to cross to reach home and descended into it, but he never reached the far side. His strength failed. A strange sleep came over him and he lay still. The snow covered him deeply.

Old Seth and Old Joe were eighty years old and too feeble to work. Their wives no longer spun wool or wove their own cloth. So the old men made an arrangement with Obed Brooks, proprietor of the general store. They deeded him some of their property, and in exchange, he supplied them with groceries and coarse broadcloth to keep them decent and warm. It then became a common sight in the village: Old Seth and Old Joe coming up slowly along the Brewster Road with a wheelbarrow, taking turns wheeling it.

In the wheelbarrow they would carry home their pork and molasses, stopping now and then to talk to someone they met along the road, and then walking on, chattering away together like two children.

Marriage Moment of Annoyance—Coconut

After many days, he said to her:

"Could you *do* something with this coconut?"

On Their Way South on Sunday Morning (They Thought)

Mark and Gail stopped to refuel their bike and themselves. But when they entered the restaurant, the woman who greeted them with menus in her hands said, "We only serve breakfast on Sunday." "But this *is* Sunday," Mark said. "Yes, so we only serve breakfast," the woman said. They were still confused.

Her statement seemed to be a negative one, a warning, as though they would not be able to have anything to eat, even though it was Sunday, and, they thought, morning.

Still, she was holding menus in her hands, as though for them.

Here is one of the problems—it is a grammar problem. The modifier "only" seems to be misplaced, so that her meaning is unclear. "We only serve breakfast on Sunday" actually could mean, "The only day we serve breakfast is Sunday. We do not serve breakfast on any other day of the week." It could also mean that the restaurant served other meals in addition to breakfast, in which case Mark and Gail could eat, no matter what the time of day. To convey what must have been her actual meaning correctly, the woman should have put the modifier "only" directly in front of the word it modified, and said, "We serve only breakfast on Sunday." Also correct, and even clearer, would have been to invert the word order so that the last phrase came first: "On Sunday, we serve only breakfast," or, even more explicitly, "On Sunday, the only meal we serve is breakfast." In fact, if she had used this inverted word order, the woman could have returned to the more casual, though incorrect, use of the modifier and said, "On Sunday, we only serve breakfast," and her meaning would have been clear enough.

The woman's emphatic statement might have seemed to indicate that Mark and Gail would not be able to eat at the restaurant, because, in fact, the restaurant served only breakfast on this day, and the hour for breakfast, despite what Mark and Gail believed, was past, since it was now early afternoon. But did the woman's confusing statement actually mean that it was too late for Mark and Gail to have something to eat? No.

It meant that although they could have something to eat, they should not expect to eat lunch. No, the restaurant was still offering breakfast. And so, after delivering her first, cautionary statement, and then repeating it, the woman more kindly showed Mark and Gail to a nice table outdoors, in the shade, on the restaurant patio, and sent a waitress to take their order.

As they ate, Mark wondered: perhaps, because his hearing was not as sharp as it had once been, he had missed the woman's intonation when she warned them about the menu restriction—maybe he did not catch the intonation that told them they could indeed have something to eat. Mark may not have taken into account the fact that the placement of "only" in a sentence has been a source of studious commentary since the eighteenth century and especially that its placement in standard spoken English is not fixed, since ambiguity is avoided through sentence stress—precisely the stress that Mark and Gail may have missed.

How long did they stay? Until their hunger was satisfied, and until they were rested and ready to continue on their way. Did they then remember to refuel their bike? They did.

Claim to Fame #1: Ezra Pound

I don't know quite how to express this. I'll try a few ways:

Pound's son Omar was the husband of my half-sister's father's niece.

My half-sister's father's niece, that is, my half-sister's first cousin on her father's side, was married to Ezra Pound's son Omar.

My half-sister's father's sister had a daughter who married Pound's son Omar.

One of the two daughters of my half-sister's father's sister Louise Margaret married Pound's son Omar.

My half-sister's aunt Louise Margaret's daughter's father-in-law was Ezra Pound.

My half-sister's aunt's daughter's father-in-law was Ezra Pound.

Later I explain this as best I can to a friend who is an expert on Pound, since I think it might interest him. He is mildly interested, but then points out that Omar was not in fact Pound's biological son.

His only biological child was one he did not acknowledge.

That child was the illegitimate daughter of Olga Rudge.

I don't mind having my facts corrected.

III

Woman Goes to Racetrack Owner

In early winter, a woman goes to the owner of a large automobile racetrack near here to talk with him about the schedule for the upcoming season. She is a gentle, kind woman, whereas the racetrack owner can be a hard man. But, perhaps in response to her, despite himself, at this meeting he is also gentle. She is going to him because her daughter wants to be married in the backyard of the family home, where she grew up, and it is close to the track—the track is just across a wide stream and beyond a patch of woods from their house. Her daughter and she are ready to decide on a date for the ceremony. They would like to know what the racing schedule is, to see if the owner can make sure there is one afternoon left clear of any races or test runs. They will then schedule the ceremony to take place on that afternoon, when the track is quiet. It is not just the noise of the track they are trying to avoid. If the ceremony were to take place on a race day, then, in the brief intervals between the announcements from the loudspeakers and the roar of the engines, the race-goers might be disturbed by the sound of the young woman's vows and the music coming through the trees.

Aging

A woman may reach the age of fifty-five and be in generally good health, not seriously ill or disabled, yet have ten things wrong with her body, by her latest count. From the top down: eyelashes, eyes, tooth, jaw, gland, left elbow, liver, unmentionable, left knee, right foot . . .

Our Strangers

1

People are strangers to me. People I don't know have habits that are nothing like my habits. These habits surprise me and yet they don't surprise other people: they are taken completely for granted. Someone belongs to the Hunt Club. Someone else is fond of Dubonnet before dinner and always knows when it is time for a drink. These people are not like me and they are not really like each other, although they seem to me more like each other than like me just because they have in common the fact that they are all strangers to me.

Then I move into an empty house, and suddenly next door to me is a stranger. I live my life and next door to me he lives his life, and because of what we have in common, we become a sort of family together. We are like a family and unlike a family, since we come together as strangers and form a temporary alliance, while family members often come to be strangers and are bound together only by blood. A neighbor becomes a sort of cousin, or parent. Or else a neighbor becomes a bitter enemy, an intolerable presence encroaching on one's land.

2

A man and his son next door to me here in the village resented me and my house so much that they covered all the windows of their house that look out on mine. This was not enough and they hung dark yellow sheets in back of their house on a clothesline, so that I couldn't see into their yard. Their anger was not satisfied and the son broke into my house while I was away in the city—not to steal, but to damage something of mine and walk into a place where he had not been invited. I heard him leave by the back door as I entered the front. I never saw him. I rarely see him. I never see the father. Sometimes, only when I am working in my garden, I hear him muttering behind the fence.

3

Another neighbor of mine has oriental rugs and I sometimes think of stealing one. She doesn't need all she has. There are larger ones in her living room and small ones running down her hallway and more in the upstairs bedroom. Most of my floors are bare. During the summer she goes away to Block Island. She sends me a postcard from Block Island. She would not think that I had stolen a rug from her, because she knows I am honest. We like to spend time together. We have dinner together.

But the very perfection of this crime that I think about makes it impossible. She would not suspect me, because I could not steal from her, and because I could not do it, I cannot do it.

4

Nearly every family in this town has had difficulties with a neighbor on one side or the other. The problems are not just the ones that prevail year after year: dogs that bark or howl; too many lights on all night long; the occasional loud music, the occasional loud party, burning brush and leaves, fireworks, or roaring all-terrain vehicles in the fields. These are annoyances that people put up with, for the most part. The more difficult problems have to do with what happens along the property lines. The shared property lines are the focus of very strong feelings.

Some of the problems are these: a man and his wife build a tiny outside deck illegally within a few feet of the property line. They won't move it. Their neighbor will no longer speak to them.

Then there is a compost pile. These people, avid gardeners, have built three large, but neatly maintained, compost piles in the far back corner, away from the road and away from their house, but bordering the neighbor's backyard. This feels to the neighbor like an insult. He will no longer speak to them.

Another town resident leaves his cats to roam freely, in and out of his back porch through a cat door. We have lost count of how many cats there are. He does not have them neutered, and they reproduce. In their wanderings they visit the yards of all the nearby residents, up and down the road. They creep through the tall grass and spray doorsteps and catch songbirds. But, as far as we know, no one has complained to him.

Once, there was a problem with a fence erected along a shared property line. Erecting the fence seemed rude, and the better-looking side was not facing the neighbors. The etiquette of erecting a fence dictates that the better-looking side of the fence should face the neighbors, as a matter of courtesy and conciliation.

A neighbor burns noxious substances in an outdoor burn barrel close to the property line. The police are called. In retaliation, the front door of the one who made the call is badly damaged.

There is one town resident who does nothing offensive along his property line, but is merely silent and hostile. Nailed to a tree trunk in his driveway is a wooden board bearing a picture of a rifle and the words *We do not call 911.*

One town resident misunderstood where the neighbor's property line was, crossed it by a foot, and planted an Asian lily in the ground there, near the edge of a stand of saplings. After the correct line was pointed out to him, he removed the lily and his neighbor posted "No Trespassing" signs on some of the trees fronting his property.

5

It is rare that neighbors, once on bad terms, find a way to improve relations, but it happens.

Our friends some distance up the road we live on, just before you cross the bridge over the brook, tell us about their neighbors, who share the driveway with them—you come to the neighbors' house first, on the left, and then you drive on up to the top of the hill, where Howard and Ginger's old farmhouse sits between two ponds. When they moved there twenty years ago, Ginger says, she and Howard had six children between them and they wanted to be alone with their children—they had moved from a sociable life in the nearby town, and they had had enough of it. They wanted peace and quiet and nothing to do with neighbors. But the little girl who lived in the house down the driveway from them was in the habit of coming up the hill and riding her bicycle here, there, and everywhere, including on the tennis court—the people who had lived here before had not minded. Ginger and Howard quickly let the neighbors know that they did not welcome this, and that was the beginning of the bad relations, Ginger said. The bad relations continued for years.

Things were not improved when they bought a horse for their youngest child, a girl. The horse kept getting loose. They decided to try an electric fence.

They spent days putting up the fence around its pasture. During this time, the horse had to remain penned up in its stall, and it became more and more restless. It was a strong, active horse. It had been a racehorse.

When at last the fence was in place, they let the horse out into the pasture. It was so full of pent-up energy and so eager to run that it ran straight into the fence. It received a powerful shock, and, in its panicked surprise, burst right through the fence and took off down to the neighbors' place. It rampaged through the neighbors' yard, out onto the road, back through the neighbors' place, into the woods and out again, and was loose for hours before it returned to the barn, tired and hungry.

The neighbors had a dog. It was a boxer with a very distinctive yelping cry. (Ginger imitates the cry.) They heard the dog often, since it was a good watchdog and notified its owners of human visitors, stray animals, thunderstorms, rainfall, and other major events.

A year after the horse escaped and returned, while bad

feeling still prevailed and the neighbors were not speaking to them, Ginger and Howard heard from a mutual acquaintance that the horse, in its trampling through the neighbors' yard, had stepped on the dog's foot and broken it, and that the treatment for the dog had amounted to $1,400. Ginger and Howard could not believe this, especially since they had not heard a peep out of the dog, normally so vocal, and since the neighbors had never said anything about it. The neighbors never gave them a bill for the dog's treatment.

But now, at last, things have changed. Howard is dying. He is still walking about, with a walker, and sitting on his porch, and his mind is there most of the time. He eats voraciously, but it goes right through him—he is not digesting his food anymore. He is skeletally thin and weak, and he has probably no more than six months to live. A woman comes in to care for him in the mornings, but Ginger must go to work, and Howard is alone for many hours of the day. At last Ginger had to ask the neighbors for help: would they check on him from time to time, she asked, reluctantly. And they do—they walk up the driveway and see if he needs anything, they bring him something to eat, sit with him and talk. The bad feeling is slowly going away.

6

Neighbors can show great kindness.

When old Johan's mind was failing, while his wife, Grace, was still bright and competent, Grace could not get any housework done, because Johan was so bored and restless. He had nothing to do but watch television, and he often grew tired of that. And so the neighbor, Gertie, would come over with little jobs for him. One of his favorites was to count out piles of pennies and fit them into the paper rolls provided by the bank. When Johan had filled all the paper rolls, Gertie would come and collect them. Sometimes she had no more pennies for him to package. Then, at home, she would secretly undo the paper rolls, pour out the pennies, and take them back to him with new paper rolls to fill.

7

My friends Jack and Cindy also have a helpful neighbor. One day when I was visiting them, they thought they had lost their parakeet forever. The parakeet would sit in the room that Jack and the bird shared and listen to him practice the tin whistle, singing and chirping without pause as long as Jack's music continued, but was otherwise untrained and, according to Jack, untrainable. Jack did not seem overly fond of the bird. However, on this day, when the bird appeared to be gone, Jack searched the most frantically and relentlessly of us all. At last, defeated and tired, we stood still in the room where he and the bird spent most of their time. When we fell completely silent, we heard a little scratching and scraping noise. Had the bird gotten inside the wall, somehow? That would be a great problem. But no, the bird had fallen in behind a row of books on a bookshelf and could not stretch its wings far enough to fly up and out. The bird was found and rescued. Jack scolded it and blamed it for its foolishness and for making him worry.

Then Jack and Cindy told me about their neighbor and the bird. They got on with their neighbor, and always had. The neighbor looked after things for them when they were not there—their house and garden, and the little guesthouse that Jack had built. The neighbor also looked after the parakeet when they went away for more than a day. A placid, retired fellow with time on his hands, he would come over, refresh the bird's food and water, and clean out the floor of its cage. Then he would sit down and make himself comfortable on the sofa in the little room, take up his newspaper, and read aloud to the bird, usually from the sports section.

8

Last year, I visited friends who live on a hillside in Vermont. The apple farmer who owned the land in back of them and to one side of them had extensive orchards and woods and some isolated groves of other trees on his property. This land was all rolling hills and fields that sloped down away from my friends' house and on and on as far as the eye could see (I thought, anyway). The orchards were on a distant hilltop.

When I was sitting with my friends and admiring the view, they told me a story. They told me how one day, when they had not been living there very long, their neighbor, the apple farmer, came over to visit them. He and they sat out on the small stone-flagged patio in back of the house where we were now sitting, away from the road. They probably had a glass of wine in hand, since, as I knew, they enjoyed a glass of wine, though they would never bring out the bottle as early as I was ready for it. They told me they were talking with their neighbor and looking out at what they could see of the landscape, through the trees. The view of the distant rolling hills—the hills that rolled on and on forever, I thought—was obscured by the clump of maples and oaks growing up high, so close to them, beyond the shared property line, on the farmer's land. After a while, the apple farmer remarked, "Your view would be a lot better without those trees." My friends, who are both very quiet people, capable of sitting quite still in company and not saying a word for minutes on end, which does unnerve me sometimes, no doubt said nothing in reply to this, and the conversation meandered on to other things. But the next morning, when my friends woke up, there were men out in back of the house, just beyond the property line. They were felling the trees. They took them all down. When they were finished, there was a wide-open view of the rolling hills. The view was indeed a lot better.

9

When I lived in the city, in one of the many apartment buildings I lived in, I had next-door neighbors whom I had never met. They were an older couple, or seemed so to me, since I was very young. We had never spoken, although their door was next to mine at the very end of the hallway. I suppose we simply never came out or went in at the same time, odd as that may seem. Then, one day, the delivery boy from the dry cleaner's came with a delivery for them when I was at home and they were out. I opened my door at the sound of his knocking and ringing, and took the hangers of plastic-wrapped clothes for them. This was in the days when people were more trusting than they are now. Later I rang my neighbors' doorbell and gave them the delivery. They were surprised and cordial. They thanked me, hesitantly. But I never encountered them again.

10

Across the hall from me, on the top floor of another building in the city, where I lived a few years later, was my neighbor Miss McAdams. She lived alone with her gray poodle. The poodle was a noisy animal who kept running around the corner of the terrace to bark at me. Miss McAdams loved her dog deeply. When we rode up and down in the elevator together, she spoke to the dog instead of to me, or perhaps the only way she could speak to me was by speaking to the dog.

Aside from this, I did not have much to do with Miss McAdams. Once, a French friend of mine was visiting and was bored and went across the hall because Miss McAdams was having a party. It was a loud party of what looked like mostly middle-aged office workers. I stayed home. My French friend drank a lot and tried to pick up an older woman there. He was forced out the door of Miss McAdams's apartment and fell into my door drunk and angry. But Miss McAdams did not hold this against me.

Another night she knocked on my door. She was crying. Something was wrong with her dog. It could not jump up onto her bed. It kept falling off the furniture. Its hind legs were paralyzed and it dragged them over the floor behind it. I sat with Miss McAdams while she waited for her brother to come and drive her to the veterinarian downtown. We had a drink together. This was the only time I saw the inside of her apartment.

After that the dog had to be carried out of the building every day to do its business. It got weaker and weaker. Finally, Miss McAdams took it back to the veterinarian downtown and he put it to sleep. That night I could hear her through the walls. She was drinking with a woman friend and crying. Every now and then she said loudly, "I'm a coward, I'm just a coward."

Sometime after that an old woman in the building died. There was a small friendly black dog named Bonnie that had to be disposed of. The dog was brought up to Miss McAdams, and she took it even though she had said she did not want another dog. Every day at the same time, after she came home from work, I could hear its toenails clicking as it ran up and down the hallway waiting for her to take it out and walk it. She seemed to like the dog, but in the elevator she talked to me now, and not to the dog.

11

The same fall a boy in our building was very ill with leukemia, though he was still going to school. He was a cheerful, plump little boy and his older brother was also cheerful and plump. I would see them playing across the street in the park. Their father was a professor at a nearby university. One day in November, the boy was too weak to get out of the school bus by himself. The driver came into the building and called up to the boy's mother on the intercom. I was in the elevator with her when she rode down to the lobby. She didn't seem to know I was there and started pounding her fists on the doors because the elevator was moving so slowly. She stopped pounding, shook her fists in the air, and then started pounding again. When the doors opened she ran out, looking angry.

Just before Christmas I went to a party given by a couple who lived in the building, an old Russian doctor and his wife. This doctor had once, in his youth, walked a mile through a snowy Russian winter to deliver the baby of a young poet. When he reached her home, he found her lying in bed on filthy sheets, smoking. She later became very famous. Her baby grew up to young manhood and was then killed fighting in the Second World War. I heard this story at the party and then, just before the party was over, someone told me that the little boy with leukemia had died.

A few days after the party I saw the boy's father, a large awkward man holding a briefcase, standing in the front hall talking to a couple of his neighbors and weeping.

Conversation Before Dinner

Husband is in pantry choosing bottle of wine.

Wife is standing next to pan full of sizzling meat.

H: [Mumble, mumble].

W (*in singsong voice*): Couldn't hear you . . .

H: [Mumble, mumble].

W (*same singsong voice*): Still couldn't hear you . . .

H (*coming out of pantry with bottle of wine*): What did you say?

W: I said I couldn't hear you—

H (*interrupting*): Are you telling me what to do again?

W (*surprised*): What?

H: Are you trying to make me feel guilty about drinking wine?

W (*innocent*): No! I was just telling you I couldn't hear what you were saying.

H: Oh.

W: What were you saying?

H: I don't remember.

Father Enters the Water

In life, he would walk into the water slowly until it reached his waist and stand there for a while, his arms out to the side, fingering the water, looking at the horizon. Then at last he would plunge forward with a great splash.

We wait. He is near us in the water, his back to us, a little hunched.
His pale, freckled arms are at his sides, his hands held just clear of the water.
Then he puts his hands together and dives. We step back.

But in death it is different: he cleaves the water with barely a ripple or a murmur, and it closes quietly over him.

Bothered Scholar on Train

Oh, can't you quiet down, please! I'm trying to read some stories in the language of Armagnac. Armagnac is a dialect of Occitan that I've never encountered before, and it isn't easy! It's hard work figuring some of the stories out, and others I can't figure out at all, even though I know French!

But this isn't French! Let me explain: Occitan is an ancient language indigenous to the south and southwest of France, and even extending down over the border, i.e., the Pyrenees mountains, into Spain. And within Occitan, which is still spoken today, by about 15 million French people, there are four main dialects—Provençal, Northern Provençal, Limousin, and Gascon, Gascony being in the southwest corner of France. So this is not French, it's the Gascony dialect of Occitan, but also, these stories that I'm reading, or trying to read, if only you would be a little quieter, are written in a particular variety of the dialect of Gascony, and that is the *patois* of Auch.

I can't define *patois* for you very easily, especially if you're talking over me, but I'll just say that it is an even more local type of speech, it's the particular way a provincial person talks in a *very small* part of a rural area of France. Actually, as I learned recently, the term *patois* is derogatory, and tends to be used by people who despise the language they're talking about.

As for Auch, Auch is a city in the very center of Armagnac. And by Armagnac I mean the territory to which the name Armagnac was extended under the old monarchy, and which corresponds more or less to the entire *département* of Gers. The inhabitants of Gers are known as Gersois, a very hard word to pronounce (the first *s* is pronounced "z" and the second is silent). Gers is named after the Gers River, which is 111 miles long, rising in the Pyrenees and running not only generally downhill, like all flowing water, but at the same time north—which you probably think of as *up*—through three *départements* altogether, before joining the Garonne River.

These stories seem to me quite lively and charming when I can figure out what is going on in them—some have to do with ghosts and graveyards, and pigs and priests. You might enjoy them too, if you weren't talking so loudly and constantly all around me. But adding to the difficulty of reading them is the fact that they were not written by a single literate individual, but are folktales that were recited out loud and copied down as they were being told. And this transcription was not done recently but in the mid-nineteenth century. Also, the stories were transcribed phonetically, the way they sounded to the person writing them down, so this person spelled the words of the stories in whatever way he liked. Some of them I can't even look up anywhere. There is no dictionary of them.

On top of all this, the book I have is a facsimile of the old 1867 edition. The type is faint in places, and pieces of some letters are missing. The publisher of this edition apologizes, saying, "The reader will please excuse, on the one hand, the slight lack of readability, and, on the other, the imperfections due to the damage inflicted by the passing decades; considering the memory of the authors and the quality of the work, it seemed suitable to reproduce it with its original characteristics."

So, please.

Encounter in Landscape

A woman in bifocals missing one tooth
asked the way
of a woman in sunglasses missing three teeth
on a cloudy day.

Betrayal (Tired Version)

Sometimes, in fact, what I want most is to be left alone. Is this because I am so extremely tired? Then, my fantasy of a relationship with another man, a man other than my husband, simply involves being left alone. My lover, who is sometimes faceless, if I haven't yet decided who he is, comes to my door and I tell him to leave—Go away. I do not even have to be polite. *Leave*. Then I can remain alone. I can rest. But of course it is an important part of the fantasy for him to want to be with me and come looking for me.

I ask myself, after all, How can I dream of anything more active if I'm so very tired? When I am so tired, I can't even manage a fantasy about having any company at all, even sitting side by side on a sofa. So I say:

Sometimes, in fact, my dearest wish is to be left entirely alone. A lover will come to the door, and I will turn him away. Go. I do not even have to be polite.

But because it still seems wrong to have, in my fantasy, a relationship with another man that is concealed from my husband, even if the fantasy is about telling the lover to go away, the fantasy itself still feels like a betrayal.

End of Phone Conversation with Verizon Adjustment Person

I say: "I guess I'd better take your name . . ."

She says: "It's Shelley . . . as in Byron, Keats, and Shelley."

"Hah! . . . I'm glad you like them, too!" I say.

"Oh, yes," says Shelley.

"I wish my name were Keats," I add, "but it's not . . ."

"I do, too!" she says. "Thank you for choosing Verizon Wireless."

An Explanation Concerning the Rug Story

Just to make sure the situation is clear:

There are two couples who are neighbors.

The woman in one couple is named Davis, and the man in the other couple is named Davis.

They are not related by blood or marriage.

They are the two indecisive ones regarding the rug (and not only the rug).

Their spouses in this particular situation are peripheral, certainly without strong opinions about the rug.

(Though it is not clear why.)

The male Davis's wife appears only in the scene in the driveway, not at the post office.

The female Davis's husband appears only once, when his observation about the rug is mentioned.

An Ant

You call this company? . . . It's no bigger than a dot.

That's not quite true—several dots. And it moves. It waves its antennae, it seems to be thinking.

They're talking about an ant.

She watches the ants when they come out onto the counter. They are nibbling at the tiny stains she has left. Or they walk up onto a slice of apple. They start off this way and that, and then change their minds. They brace themselves when she blows on them. They sometimes appear to be running off in alarm. They gather around and drink at a drop of water.

She has realized that they are company, of a kind. She has told him this.

So the question is whether something that is only as big as the broken tip of a lead pencil can be called company.

If there is just one, she says, it can seem like company. But if they spread out (like a constellation) over the wall above the sink, they do not seem so much like company. They have each other.

Especially when she's feeling peaceful, when she's feeling quiet, then an ant is good company.

But if you think you can call it company, can you call it a companion?

That's a little harder.

Still, there was the story that Fritz and Hildegard told us:

One year, at Christmastime, during the war, before they came to America, there wasn't much to eat. They had to stay in their apartment most of the time. They didn't have children yet. They were frightened, and lonely. Every mealtime, when they sat down to eat, a fly would come buzzing around, landing here and there on the food. They became used to the fly. Eventually, it became a sort of companion. They would put out some food for it on its own plate.

And then, on Christmas Day, they found the fly lying dead on the table. They were stricken. She cried. Or they both cried.

But years later—remember?—we met their son down at the Colmans', and when we reminded him of this story, he made a face. Remember? He shrugged and said it might not be true.

I never knew exactly what he meant. That his parents had made it up? That his mother thought she remembered it, and his father went along with her?

That was the son with the Zuni wife. We liked her better than him.

Yes. But she wasn't Zuni, she was Tewa.

Still, it was a good story. It could have been true.

Do you remember, you thought they might leave you their ninety acres of woods? Just because they were estranged from their children?

Yes, but they did like us. And we helped them with their harvest once, remember? They were so old by then. They were in a panic about the vegetables. We all went over and helped them get their vegetables in. It was my birthday—that's why both kids were home.

We weren't harvesting, we were weeding.

Maybe you're right—they couldn't keep up with the weeds.

You're always imagining that people are going to leave you their money or their property—people you don't really know very well.

Only four times.

And did any of them ever leave you anything?

One of them hasn't been dead very long—just a couple of weeks. They haven't read her will yet.

Gramsci

A friend is talking to her, on the phone, about pessimism of the intellect and optimism of the will. They both think that because of what she has been reading over the holidays, this may now be what she has.

On a notepad, while they are talking, she writes down "Gramsci."

After she hangs up, he comes along, glances suspiciously at the notepad, and reads the word. He is afraid her friend has been recommending an expensive line of clothes.

"What's Gramsci?" he says. "A designer?"

"No." She wants to startle him: "An Italian Marxist." They don't often use the word *Marxist* in their home.

He walks away, but she can see from his expression that he is not convinced.

Pardon the Intrusion

Does anyone have experience resurfacing porcelain?

Is anyone interested in bagged leaves from the past winter?

I'd be grateful if someone could recommend a good dentist and/or periodontist in the area. Thanks!

Can anyone recommend a dermatologist in the area?

Could anyone recommend a chiropractor in the area?

Pardon the intrusion, but some of us will be living in a hot residence hall and would like to borrow some fans, preferably oscillating.

Does anybody want to watch the HD production of “The Merry Widow” with Renée Fleming?

An umbrella was left behind after the meeting yesterday. It is being held at the information desk.

Would anyone like this toddler bed?

Pardon the intrusion, but I’m in need of 6–8 large moving boxes.

Kayak for sale. If interested, please call Betty.

Trusty iMac available. It’s working fine. Articles just write themselves.

Does anyone have any personal connections to a local dairy farm?

If you have tickets to “Oklahoma” that you are not going to use, I am looking to buy some.

Has anyone had good experience with a company that could help to load and unload a truck?

This easel (see below) is fully adjustable. It can be used horizontally for watercolor work, and tilts forward for pastels.

The couch comes with two matching brown pillows and is fairly low to the ground. Have a lovely holiday weekend!

Thank you for all who have expressed an interest, but the bookshelf sold.

Pork butts claimed. Thanks, guys!

I am in need of a sturdy chair for a wedding on July 23rd, one that will hold a very pregnant bride during the Hora. Does anyone have such a chair that could be borrowed for this occasion?

We are looking for a mature female caregiver. Must have a car.

Free rooster. A surprise amongst our new flock of hens, he is about three months old.

Pardon the intrusion. Is anyone in need of brown expanding folders?

Greetings. I'll be going out of town in early August and my turtle is interested in paying someone to stop by 3–4 times to drop some lettuce off with him. Please contact me on his behalf if you know someone who might be interested.

Exterminator needed, especially one who specializes in bedbugs. We are stuck in Italy, and this is a very time-sensitive matter.

Pardon the intrusion. The folders have been taken.

Hello. I'm working on a new large photograph and looking for small roses from the garden for the piece. Also hoping for some quinces!

We would love to have help unloading a truck at our new house.

Painting crew needed in August to help me stain my log house.

Pardon the intrusion—we have a few items to sell, among them: one glass-topped desk, one dumbbell set, and one Founding Fathers board game.

Does anyone have a British-to-U.S. plug adapter to lend or sell? The appliance is British, the wall outlet U.S.

Our three visiting international scholars have packages that appear to be lost.

We are in the search of at least 40 gently loved 3-ring binders for our new students. We would prefer anything from 1/2 inch to 2 inch, but are open to what you may have.

Two female musicians would like to sublet a dog-friendly apartment.

We are looking for a small package currently MIA. Is it hiding in a dusty corner of your office?

Pardon the intrusion, but I and the Professor have a surfeit of borage. Any suggestions?

We are still looking for a small package addressed to Lourdes.

Thank you all for your input regarding the gastroenterologist.

We are missing a package that was sent to the archivist. It contains a photograph of the South H. Drinking Society Farewell Party. (Francis is with the clock and the pipe.)

We have a pair of extra tickets to "Love Is Crazy" on Saturday—selling them as a pair.

Seeking somewhere to move into, such as a cabin in back of something large.

I am hoping to make walnut ink with my students. Does anyone have a walnut tree who would be willing to part with their nuts?

I am hoping to find someone who has experience in doing makeup for a wedding in October. There will be a total of 4 girls getting their makeup done.

Seek chimney mason for neglected chimney in old house.

Visiting scholar from Hungary seeks place to stay that is simple and clean.

Wanted: rubber ducks. I will pick up.

Seeking somewhere to move into that is along a stream somewhere. I don't mind inconvenience.

Dear colleagues, my daughter's calculator died.

I have a box of inkjet cartridges, free to a good home.

Anyone looking to offload a rooftop cargo carrier?

Does anyone have used binders?

Seek local person handy with lifting heavy objects.

I have two more tickets for "Love Is Crazy."

Nuts found.

Any suggestions for someone to fix a broken water pump?

Looking for two strong and careful individuals to move some large pieces of furniture between locations.

We are a couple of language tutors trying to get to a show.

If anyone is missing a rooster, please call Marie.

Can anyone recommend an honest stamp dealer?

We are looking for a good and reasonable local piano tuner for a very old German piano.

We are looking for a travel version of go.

We are looking for unwanted egg cartons.

Creditable squash and tennis player looking for partner.

I am a pianist and would like a violinist to play the Kreuzer Sonata with.

Did you lose your glasses? I found this pair (see pic below). If you can read this, please come by and pick them up.

Pardon the intrusion. We have a wide range of moving boxes, wrapping paper, bubble wrap, and so on, for anyone interested.

Egg cartons found! Thanks to all who responded!

Does anyone have a viola that I could borrow or rent for this weekend? It will be used for fiddle music not classical.

Telescope taken.

Please pardon the intrusion. We are moving house and are in need of boxes for packing. Please let me know if you have any to spare. Thanks.

Do you want to sell me your car? Something with a little panache preferred.

My son's iMac keyboard no longer types the letter "o"—anyone have an old iMac keyboard kicking around that you don't use?

My daughter recently dropped her (almost-one-year-old) iPhone 5c and the screen is badly cracked. We tried replacing the screen but that caused more problems. Now we're looking for a used iPhone to which to transfer her account.

My son dropped (or more accurately, threw) his cell phone and it no longer works. Does anyone have a used, working, Verizon cell phone to sell?

Looking to sell my Subaru Impreza Outback Sport, overall good condition except some traces of pine sap.

Can anyone recommend a knowledgeable arborist? A big branch has recently fallen off my large front-yard tree, blocking traffic on the street.

Looking for a Lithuanian-speaker to help translate some papers.

We are still drowning in moving boxes—if you need some high quality, of any size, please be in touch.

Newly formed Road Runners Club looking for more members. We meet under the water tower every Thursday and start running sharply at 7 pm.

Cast-iron wok. Practically new.

Thick cozy orange-red rug for sale, great condition, daughter got tired of it. See attached photo.

Cast-iron wok sold.

Would like to sell some furniture! See pics below. From smoke-free home with one cat.

Ulster Ballet Company is hosting a Sip and Paint fundraiser this Wednesday at Christina's Restaurant. Paint with a little wine or soda, whichever you prefer.

Accordion player needed. Please contact Marie.

Hi, I have a mold infestation in my attic and am looking for a mold remediation contractor.

Does anyone have a recommendation for a dentist in the area?

French tutor needs ride to Boston to visit a friend. Will pay for gas and bring cookies and French music.

Thank you for all the dentist recommendations.

I have a fairly large Australian Tree Fern. My house does not have enough light for it to winter over. Anyone with indoor space and good light?

All hanging folders have been spoken for.

I'm offering a vintage Revere slide projector with 6 boxes of slide trays, still works!

Any suggestions for a good window person?

For sale: Audio-Technica unidirectional moving coil dynamic microphone in original box, plus stand.

My son needs a piano. Does anyone have an upright that stays in tune they aren't using?

My daughter recently began violin lessons and needs a half size bow. She is growing like a weed and I know that she will soon need a 3/4 size. She is a sweet, responsible girl.

Does anyone have an old red trench coat they would like to get rid of? My niece is looking for one.

Does anyone know of a landscaper or handyperson who does brush-hogging?

Does anyone have a recommendation for a competent non-charlatan podiatrist in the area?

For sale: rollerblades, women's size 6, black, including knee and elbow guards, and instructions. Used once.

There is a wonderful new florist in town. If you have never dropped in, I encourage you to do so! She has quite an eye.

I wonder if anyone could recommend a local dentist?

Does anyone have any plastic magazine/booklet holders that you are not using any longer?

Hi, everyone! I have a brown leather couch with an ottoman and a gray fabric chair for sale. Photos attached. Have a beautiful day!

Do you still need moving boxes? We just moved and have a fair amount.

Can anyone recommend a great restaurant in Boston?

We have 8 medium size boxes available. Please advise if you're interested.

I am seeking a reliable and trustworthy person in the area who can repair antique clocks. Thanks for any suggestions!

So sorry for the second intrusion, but I am really hoping to get rid of my TV before I move on Sunday morning. Please make an offer . . .

Boxes have been taken. Thanks!

We need short-term housing for a large group of 20 artists who will be on site in January—any leads?

Just in time for the holidays, I'm looking for a way to machine-quilt a queen-sized quilt. Thanks in advance for any leads.

Anyone know a bakery still selling apple pies for Thanksgiving?

Any typewriter collectors out there? Or know any?

Sharper Image Sanitizing Steamer in original box—never used.

My neighbors are selling their car and I offered to post the ad. They are trustworthy folks.

Does anyone know anyone who would like to house and housecat sit in December? Our person just fell through.

We found about 6 pounds of plaster of Paris with the binding and petroleum jelly in our storage. Yours for picking up.

Postdoc seeks housing: Humanities postdoc fellow looking for relaxed living situation, private or shared. Friendly and respectful.

Ariens 926 Pro snowblower for sale with heated handles.

We are letting go of yet another bed.

Plaster of Paris claimed!

I'm having a little apartment sale with several items for sale including men's shoes, yarn, and luggage pieces.

Anyone know of a good real estate agent? Mine keeps telling me he doesn't want to show me houses for one reason or another and has been extremely flaky.

Mahogany soprano ukulele by Ohana with carrying case. In perfect condition, barely touched.

Ukulele taken! Thank you.

Dark brown loafers and travel wallet taken! Other shoes, including these boat shoes (worn once) still available!

I need to have a small piece of art photographed digitally. Your place or mine. Thanks!

My niece is selling her washer and dryer. See picture below.

I'm selling this Litter Robot II automatic self-cleaning litter box (see below).

Wanted: ukulele. Is anyone looking to sell?

We're looking for a responsible animal lover to take care of our energetic dog (and three low-maintenance cats).

We are looking to collect as many plastic water bottles as possible (with lids!) in the next two weeks. Have some lying around?

Seeking pianist to work with to add songs to my Audition Book. If you are interested, please contact me.

Pardon the intrusion. We are looking for empty water dispenser bottles (the large, multi-gallon, blue-tinted kind).

To everyone who responded to my inquiry about plumbers, thank you! There was a resounding endorsement of Watertight.

Greetings, Does anyone in the community have a decent quality professional French horn they want to let go of?

Comfy chair and paper lantern are spoken for, but the other items are still available.

Good morning! If you are interested in learning Spanish with a native speaker, I have many years of experience teaching both neutral Latin American accent and Castilian!

A friend is looking to rent a house in the area. Should be near a town so his mom can walk to church, with a yard (fenced or unfenced) and allows a dog who is 60 pounds.

I have some lovely green dishes made in very early 20th century China that unfortunately test positive for lead. What can I do with them?

Can anyone recommend a reputable radon mitigation contractor in the area? Thank you!

Do you have a 1- or 2-burner hotplate I could borrow tomorrow? I'd return it to you at the end of the day. Lemme know!

Thanks to all who gave me names of radon mitigation contractors.

Hotplate found! Thanks.

Looking for a used high-end serger. Let me know if you have one that has been collecting dust.

Hello everyone! I have mistakenly received a box of safety green reflective jackets (size medium). I did not order these jackets. If you ordered these jackets, please let me know. Please also send proof that you actually ordered them.

Looking for drainage contractor: a contractor in the area who specializes in drainage. Thanks.

Hi, and sorry for the intrusion. Does anyone know anyone that has a forklift with operator that I could hire for a few hours this coming weekend? Thanks in advance.

The sale continues: 2 large bins and 1 medium bin; 3 blue medium bins (I will clean these); variety of small bins; beautiful handcrafted wooden coat hook; 2 snowboards; 1 beach boogie board; 2 blue sleds; 1 Chagall lithograph; large luggage (white marks are scuffs, not mold) with leopard print inside; various canvas tote bags; faux sheepskin; furry pillow; skull pillow; heavy chrome toilet paper holder; frappe machine used once; handcrafted rolling wooden dog (tail moves) and wooden Pooh Halloween door decoration (Piglet plays peekaboo); 2 Van Gogh prints in great frames; game of Mancala.

We are looking for nurses interested in working this summer at a local Extreme Ballet camp. Email us for details.

Seeking one rooster: A fox recently decimated our chicken flock. Does anyone have an extra rooster they want to get rid of? He will be free range and happy with Red, our sweet chicken, and goats for company.

I am selling my old Circus Trunk. It's in good condition, and you can lock it.

Hello, just a friendly warning, if you or your loved ones need to see a vascular specialist, do NOT see Dr. X. in the Vascular Group in K. VERY dismissive and rude.

Thanks to all the rooster responders! Our girl will have a sweetheart soon!

Lantern and flag for sale, $10 each. Lantern uses a normal lightbulb. Full-sized flag, ready to hang!

FREE: Well-used 2 red drums from drum kit. Tom-tom covered with dark blue carpet.

If anyone has an oboe that they could lend/give/rent for a young student looking to try it out over the summer that would be great. Please let me know. Thanks.

We're looking for a fake fireplace to borrow for a show, hopefully that looks a bit like this one (see below).

Looking for fake cooked turkey for the school drama club production of "Oliver." Does anyone have one to lend?

Anyone have leads for getting a large fake bird resembling a turkey vulture (including featherless red head)—this will be for outdoor use.

An effigy is a dead or fake dead animal that is hung in an area to deter that specific species from congregating.

- Effigies are extremely effective at deterring (black) vultures from using an area if displayed properly.
- Effigies need to be hung high enough to be seen from a distance.
- Effigies should be displayed by hanging the bird upside down by their feet with the wings spread to be most effective.

Good morning—We have several pounds of Nutro brand diet chicken-based dog food to give away—our dog does not like it.

Thanks! Fake turkey found. Come see "Oliver," the weekend of March 24th!

I'm looking for an adoptive family for this turtle!

Dog food is gone: Thanks to all who responded.

I am giving away a zither in very good condition with two manuals and an extra pack of strings. Please contact me if you're interested.

Hello all, I am looking for someone to stay with my delightful elderly beagles.

I have a friend coming into town who needs just a simple, clean room (for one adult) and access to a bathroom. Any suggestions are welcome.

Zither found a home, thank you.

I am looking for one old black academic gown that someone would be willing to give away. Tattered, torn or patched is no problem.

Good morning. I am hoping to trade someone American dollars for euros at an exchange rate of 1 euro to 1.13 dollars. I am looking for 100–200 euros. Thank you.

I am looking for someone local who works on outboard motors. Ours seems to need a new impeller.

Hi, Folks: I'm organizing a jamming event this Friday. Need more electric hot plates. Can I borrow yours for 1 day?

Two goldfish which were bought as very small fish for a five gallon tank and have grown to 3 and 4 inches are getting too large for the tank. Free to anyone who will come and get them.

Seek moving "men": Need help from two strong backs on Monday, to move two pieces of furniture down a narrow staircase.

Yearling turtle for adoption! It eats sliced turkey and will probably learn to eat a good-quality commercial turtle food. Proper turtle care requires some ultraviolet light, clean water, and a couple of mineral supplements.

Pardon the intrusion here. Any recommendations for a local and reliable tuck-pointer?

Seeking old-style card file cabinet with drawers—inside width of drawer must be slightly greater than six inches (this is for storing paper packets containing specimens of mosses and lichens).

Hi, all. We are in the market for a new car, preferably in wilderness green. We want to see what wilderness green looks like. If anyone owns one and is willing to let us look at it, we'd be much obliged.

We still have flotation vests to give away!

I am looking for a drum kit (adult size) for my son. If you have one, please let me know. He is just starting out, so I am not looking for anything too pricey.

Our office is giving away our small Keurig coffeemaker (along with a box of pods).

Available: Hose cart, with hose—looks like this (see below).

Coffeemaker is taken, thank you!

Hose cart spoken for.

Area resident is looking to find a new home for 100–200 indoor plants that are 40+ years old. Plants include: cactus, begonias, money plants, ferns and Norfolk Island pines.

We have 5–6 dozen bud vases that used to be centerpieces for a dinner that we don't need anymore. Free to whoever wants them. Or a portion of them.

A few items for sale: Five-piece drum set with two cymbals and stands, PEACE brand, $100. Cruzer by Crafter electric guitar, yellow, $75. Rabbit hutch, two levels, three rooms and platform, $75.

Eggs and goat meat for sale. The girls were very busy this week, despite the heat. The goat meat may taste of basil.

Bud vases gone: Congrats to M., who will be using them at her upcoming wedding!

Looking for twin mattress–anyone have a decent one they are aching to part with?

I'm looking for two people and a truck to move a couple of items including an upright piano.

I need someone to clean the gutters on my house, help clean my gutters, or hold the ladder while I clean the gutters.

I am in need of a really skilled local animal behaviorist/dog trainer to help with some behavior issues we're having with our dog. Any suggestions will be most appreciated!

We need more nesting swallows for a study—do you have a swallow nesting on your property?

Looking for the leaves of a Sweet Gum Tree for a very hungry Luna Moth caterpillar. If you have a Sweet Gum Tree or know where I can find one, I, and the caterpillar, would be grateful.

I'd be indebted to any of you who can recommend to me a handyman for my apartment in the Rectory.

Thanks for the outpouring of messages directing me to more nearby Sweet Gum Trees than I ever imagined. Caterpillar is feasting.

I'm beginning to plan a family trip to Hawaii. Is there anyone out there with lots of knowledge who would be willing to chat with me about Hawaii?

I have a couple pounds of bird seed to give away, including a mix specifically for cockatiels. Please let me know if you're interested.

Thanks for your interest, folks. The seeds have been claimed.

University of Chicago graduation gown in excellent condition. $20.

Free huge soft-sided suitcase that I'd like to give away. The zipper is a little finicky, but otherwise it's fine.

I'm looking for a tall bookcase.

Free rooster to a good home. Beautiful, if a bit cocky. 5 months old, Ameraucana.

Hello all, from a notary: I am a notary in need of a notary that can notorize a quit claim deed.

Forgive the intrusion, but I'm in need of alterations on my mother-of-the-groom dress! Can anyone recommend someone? Thank you!

For the mother of the groom in search of a seamstress: There is a nice Korean lady in the alley by the bagels, the one that leads to the back of the movie theater. (The tailor was named Jin, but Jin retired. The place is still called Jin—I believe.)

Sorry for this question, but does anyone know of a preferably small and quiet banjo I might borrow or rent for 2 weeks? My banjo player is arriving from France with no banjo. Apologies for the intrusion!

I am looking for old newspapers for wrapping up items to securely pack.

We are searching for a used washing machine for our home upstate. Cosmetics are not a concern.

Spare twin bed available—inflatable bed on legs. Legs unfold as bed inflates, then deflates and folds up again automatically.

Does anyone have six clean bricks?

Hands on the Wheel

I thought the booklet said hands at 10 and 2 on the wheel. But maybe that's because I like to drive with my hands at 10 and 2. But the booklet actually says: hands at 9 and 3. Well, my husband usually drives with his hands at 11 and 1, which makes me nervous. And sometimes—even worse—at 7 and 5. Or, when he's really relaxed, just at 5.

Heron in the Headlights

(*Last Sunday*)

–Any wildlife reports?

–Yes, actually! I was driving down this winding road into town and I saw a great blue heron, right in the middle of the road!

–(*Pause*) Was this near water?

–No, I couldn't see water anywhere. There were woods on both sides of the road, right up to the road. It was very strange.

–What was it doing?

–It was just standing there.

–Was it eating anything off the road?

–No. Anyway, I think they only eat live fish. You usually see them standing in water and watching for fish.

–I know. What did you do? Did you stop?

–No, I just slowed down as I got closer. I didn't want to honk and scare it.

—What did it do?

—Well, it walked away down the road in front of me, at the side of the road—

—It walked?

—Yes, I think it walked quickly, I don't think it ran. Finally it flew up a few feet—it had huge wings—and then down into a deep ditch between the trees and the road. The ditch was very deep. I couldn't see it down there at all. I was worried about what it would do after I went by. I was worried that it would go back up into the road. I don't know what it was doing there. I've never seen them away from water.

—Maybe there was something wrong with it.

(*This Sunday*)

—Any wildlife reports?

—*(Pause)* Well, did I tell you about the heron I saw in the road?

—Yes, you told me about that. You could write a story about it. You could call it "Heron in the Headlights."

—But it wasn't in my headlights. I didn't have the headlights on. It was in the daytime. *(Pause)* I could call it "Heron in the Middle of the Road."

—But that doesn't have the same alliteration.

–But it wasn't at night. It was in the daytime.

–Writers don't have to tell the truth.

–But actually, I could call it that, and then say the headlights weren't actually on–

–You didn't hear me. I said writers don't have to be honest. I was being provocative.

–That's not provocative. I mean–

–Oh. (*Laughs*)

–I know writers don't have to be honest. I could call it "Heron in the Headlights" anyway, and then explain that actually it was in the daytime.

Marriage Moment of Annoyance—Insurance

She was trying to explain something to him.

What she said was confusing, contradictory, and a little incoherent.

"You're like that *insurance document*!" he said to her.

Marriage Moment of Annoyance—Mumble

"[Mumble, mumble]."

"I can't hear you."

"Do you want to hear me?"

"No."

Not Yet Ring Lardner

I said to him that I had been trying to write a story in a Ring Lardner sort of style. He asked me what a Ring Lardner sort of style was. Ring Lardner was a comic writer, I said. He wrote back in the 1920s about your average sort of guy, a middlebrow kind of American—though back then the average sort of middlebrow guy was not like what he is now.

This wasn't a very good description. But I had already lost him anyway—you have to get his attention with the first few words, and then keep it.

A couple of days later, I read him my story.

He said there was no beginning, no end, and no plot. He asked if that was the way Ring Lardner would have written it.

Well, no, I said. I'm still working on it.

Years ago, in a book I took out from the local library, I found a letter that was just like a monologue by a Ring Lardner character. The guy was writing from Florida to his buddy, and it was about going to spring training and about his wife's health. I kept the letter, it's somewhere in the house, but I've never been able to find it again. The more time goes by that I can't find it, the more it seems to me, in my memory, a perfect Ring Lardner story.

On the Train to Stavanger

Two of the things I will do on this train ride, I think, as I settle down in my seat, are look out the window at the scenery and listen to conversations around me, hoping to improve my understanding of spoken Norwegian.

I lean forward to listen to the couple who are sitting in the seats in front of me, but then they stop talking. I turn to my left to look out the window, but then the train enters a tunnel. I lean forward again to listen to the conversation in front of me, which has resumed. The couple exchange a few remarks that I don't understand. Then, at the next station, one of them stands up, says goodbye to the other, and gets off. I understand the word for "goodbye." I turn to my left again to look out the window, but the window has fogged over.

Another pair get on, put their things down in the empty

seats in front of me, walk away to another car to buy coffee, come back, sit down, laugh together, and start babbling. I lean forward to listen, though they are perhaps talking too fast for me. But abruptly, now, he has his laptop open and she has her iPhone in hand, and they stop talking.

Then three people, across the aisle and two seats ahead, start to chatter to one another, but they are too far away for me to distinguish a single word. After that, all at once, around me, everyone starts chattering and talking over one another so that I can make out nothing. Then, abruptly, everyone falls silent.

While this is happening, I think with regret how I could also have taken pictures out the window. There is one nice little shallow valley, for instance, with a white house, a red barn, dark woods in the background, a lake in front, and the sun shining on it all. But I have not brought my camera. After that, there are fir trees, a scrubby hillside, and sheep grazing. Then there is, between Egersund and Bryne, some bare, rocky, scrubby terrain that feels high up, and I think we are on a mountaintop, because I have no idea of the geography here. It turns out that we are not on a mountaintop but down by the sea. I could have brought with me a detailed map in order to follow our route, but I forgot to prepare one.

It is less populated here, not really at all, even by animals—which I know are called *dyr* in Norwegian. The rocks in the fields are not so different from sheep in the fields. I could have photographed them, but I have not brought even my iPhone.

How Sad?

How sad am I really?
Only one of my eyes is weeping.

Crepey

A long time ago, when I was young, I reported in my journal that my mother, who was old, said, laughing, that when she was my age she was afraid her eyelids were getting *crepey.* I was twenty-nine when I wrote down what she had said, and she was seventy-three. I did not know if my own eyelids were crepey. Now, as I read what I wrote down then, I am seventy-two, almost the age she was. As for my mother, she is gone, upstairs in a jar. Her eyelids, too, mixed in with the rest, are now ash.

A Mother's Devotion

I'd sacrifice my right arm to see him well and happy.
Well, maybe not my right arm.
But certainly my left.

IV

On a Winter Afternoon

The first one to go to sleep is the large gray tiger cat. He lies stretched out on a green blanket on the back of an armchair under a lamp.

The man sits in the armchair wearing his reading glasses and reading a book.

The second one to go to sleep is the large black cat. He is curled up on a dark blue blanket on the back of the sofa. The cushion under him is so soft that he is lying in a deep hollow, nearly invisible against the dark blue.

The woman is sitting at the end of the sofa close to the black cat, who, without opening his eyes, began to purr when she sat down. She is reading a magazine and taking notes in a little brown notebook.

The third one to go to sleep, after a quiet half hour, is the man, who has taken off his glasses, put down his book, folded his arms, and tipped his head back and to the side, facing away from the window. The gray cat has placed one forepaw on his shoulder.

The last one to go to sleep is the woman, who has put her pen and notebook next to her on the sofa, let the magazine rest open and facedown over her chest, and tipped her head forward.

In the midst of the silence, now, only the heating unit throbs nearby in the kitchen, bringing a little warmth into the house.

Interesting Personal Vegetables

In Indonesia, years ago, domestic servants collected and saved pieces of paper discarded by the household. They would make little bundles of them and sell them to market vendors for wrapping their produce. Among the odd pieces of paper would sometimes be a blue aerogram letter. And so, now and then, your *bawang putih* or your *buncis* would come home wrapped in someone else's personal mail.

Second Drink

She knows the alcohol is kicking in
when she thinks, wistfully,
"Dear old Shakespeare!"

Commentary on "Interesting Personal Vegetables"

In the first version of this story, the vegetables I named were ones I found when searching "Indonesian vegetables" on the internet. I thought I was quite careful, and yet it turned out that the two names I found were not good choices. I don't know the Indonesian language at all, so to me a word was just a set of letters. The editor of the magazine to whom I sent the story did not know Indonesian either, so he could not have caught my errors. But just to make sure, I sent the story to a cousin who has lived in Indonesia and is familiar with both its language and its vegetables. She said that the first term I used, *bawang merah*, was the name of a kind of red onion, the sweeter kind, and that the onion would not be wrapped at all. She suggested *bawang putih* instead, which is garlic and would be wrapped. The second term I used, *kunci*, she said, was "key." I did not know whether she meant "key" in the sense of "crucially important," though that seemed unlikely, or the sort of key you use to open a door. I wrote back asking her, and she said she meant "door key." What she thought might have been wrapped in a blue aerogram letter was not a *kunci* but *buncis*, green beans. Now all is correct, in the story, and I could include the fact that my cousin was the one who received the unexpected aerogram. But I am also left with the image of the surprising door key (a large old iron one) wrapped in a blue aerogram letter somewhere deep in the basket among the vegetables.

Claim to Fame #4: Sally Bowles

My mother's second husband, after their divorce, married the nightclub singer and writer Jean Ross, model for Sally Bowles in the musical *Cabaret*. Their relationship resulted in a daughter, my half-sister's half-sister.

A Person Asked Me About Lichens

A person asked me, had I ever written about lichens? He thought I was the kind of person who would be interested in lichens and enjoy thinking about them. He judged that because he knew of my interest in moss, seeds, pollen, leaves, soil, insects such as wasps, ants, ladybugs, and sawflies, and also spiders, particularly daddy longlegs, who have such very small heads to contain intelligence and such thin legs to contain anything like muscles. It was perfectly true that I would be interested in lichens, but the fact was that I had paid very little attention to them up to then. There are lichens growing on my apple trees and crab apple trees, and I had worried that this was a bad sign. A friend who used to grow apple trees professionally told me I did not have to worry about the lichens growing on the trees. I had only that summer become particularly interested in the wildflowers that came up in my yard, and in fact in all the wild plants that came up—most of which flowered, of course, sooner or later, though in some cases inconspicuously. Along with that interest, or coming soon after it, I began to pay more attention to mushrooms. I had always noticed the mushrooms that sprouted, suddenly, overnight, here and there in spots of their own choosing, often after a rain or some prolonged damp weather, sometimes in spots that puzzled me, that I would not have chosen, had I been a mushroom, such as at the very edge of my asphalt driveway—though, of course, when I thought about it, had I really been that type of mushroom I would have chosen precisely that spot. Other spots made more sense to me, though I know very little about mushrooms, only, perhaps, that they are actually the fruit of some sort of long underground stems—in other words, that they are only the outward, surface sign of a much larger living organism, an idea that is a little frightening. But of course what happens below the surface of the soil is very complex and on a large scale, or I should say on a small scale, but vast, if that makes any sense, invisible to us and mostly unknown to most of us. In any case, after years of only noticing mushrooms, usually admiring, sometimes marveling at them, I learned that without much trouble I could grow them myself. I thought I would need a rotten log or a pile of wood chips, which I had, and some spores which I could order to be delivered here. I decided not to do it this year, since I was busy already with various new plantings, but I would do it the following year. I had also been given a small book by a dear friend that showed different types of mushrooms, with clear line drawings and descriptions, and symbols indicating whether the mushroom was safe to eat. I began to look up in this book the mushrooms that appeared in the yard. I was not sure of my identifications, so I took photos of the mushrooms and sent them to two other friends of mine who are good at identifying mushrooms, the husband slightly more practiced than the wife, who will make her own identification but then defer to him to verify it. And he will, in turn, then venture an identification, sometimes waiting until he has his full range of books available, then often agreeing with his wife, but then cautioning me that he can't be sure without a spore print. I had never heard of a spore print before this year. As it happened, the mushrooms that came up in the yard and that my friends identified for me were all highly poisonous except for the last ones, which sprouted in the relatively fresh wood chips under one of the old apple trees and which they identified with almost complete certainty as a kind of puffball. They went on to say that puffballs were edible, but that, even so, I should not eat these. Then, after the season for growing was past, and without my asking, a young friend presented me with a mushroom-growing kit. It consisted of a bag tightly packed with little plugs impregnated with mushroom spawn, along with a leaflet of instructions and a catalog of interesting fungus-related items. The leaflet warned you not to insert your plugs until you had given the plug spawn a chance to recover from their long, undoubtedly bumpy journey, during which the mycelia might have temporarily collapsed. You would know they had recovered by their whitish, fuzzy appearance. I'm not sure what mycelia are, yet. I also learned that you do not set your plugs of mushroom spawn in just any piece of wood, as I had thought, but that you need oak for one type, beech for another, ash for yet another, and so on. My plugs contain the spawn of shiitake mushrooms, good for a beginner since they are rated easy to grow, and for them I will need logs of oak. I think I know where I can get oak. A young farmer friend told me this past summer that his family owns a large forest that includes fifty acres almost exclusively of oak. Meanwhile, since it is winter, I need to put my packet of plugs and spawn in the refrigerator, preferably in the vegetable bin, and wait until temperatures outdoors are above 40 degrees. I have done that and will wait. I will have all the rest of the winter to read and reread the leaflet of instructions and decide if I can ask my young farmer friend for some oak logs. When I take the plugs out, I will observe them, as instructed, and not insert them into the log until their mycelia have acclimated to room temperature. After the person said he guessed I might be interested in lichens, of course I immediately did become interested in lichens. He said I was probably a lichen-curious person, though I was in fact not yet a lichen-curious person, until he said this. He thought I might already be engaged on a lichen-related project. He knew, or thought he knew, that I looked at things closely, even small things. Now he was asking me to look more closely at lichens. I started by looking more closely at the lichens on my crab apple tree, the one near the side door. The landscape of this tree, now that the leaves are off, is bright with small red apples, dark twigs, and pale blue-green lichens. They are in fact beautiful, in color and form, though so small. They are growing not only on the crab apple tree branches, but also on some of the flagstones in the lawn. The lichens nearly cover one of the flagstones entirely. If they grow on stones, I have to wonder, as I've never wondered before, what they eat. I went on a forest walk with my grown-up son and brought home a small piece of bark that had fallen off a tree and was lying in the path, with what seemed to be two kinds of lichens growing on it. Both are a pale, milky green, one more yellowish and one more bluish. They grow in different patterns. The more yellowish one, if I look very closely, resembles miniature cilantro leaves, greatly bleached and growing so close together, or overlapping, that you can't see the bark under them. The other, the bluish one, a little larger though also very small, resembles seaweed, with spaces between its flat antler-shaped tendrils where the dark gray bark shows through. I don't know much, at this point, about lichens. I don't know if these patches of growth on the piece of tree bark, now that the bark is separated from its tree, are dead or alive, or if, by bringing them home and indoors, I have ended their lives. Soon after bringing them in, I put them away somewhere, safe from the cat, who is an indoor cat and therefore intensely curious about anything that comes into the house from outside, particularly anything natural, and now I'm not sure where they are. I have not yet begun reading about lichens. I don't know if lichens will be a part of the permaculture gardening effort that I began making this year. I doubt it, though I've been learning that almost everything I see in my yard has some role to play in that great interactive system. For instance, my son asked, the other day, skeptically,

Do we really need wasps? I knew we did, but could think of only one reason at the moment, knowing there were other reasons, depending, however, on the type of wasp. My questions, at the moment, are about lichens. For instance, do they eat the mineral in the stone? Or do they eat something in the air? I know I could quickly and easily find answers to some of these questions, but I like to continue to wonder about something first, in order to give some exercise to my intelligence, such as it is. Now, just recently, as it happens, several other members of my family requested gifts of books on nature. One is interested in small fish, one in mosses, and one, coincidentally, also in lichens—I haven't yet asked her why. When I ordered these books from my local independent bookstore, I also ordered a book on lichens for myself. I found that the bookseller, when we began to talk about this, was herself very enthusiastic about lichens, especially how beautiful they are in winter, when there is such a limited number of things to see on a walk in the woods. She has noticed many more kinds of lichens than I have, so far. I have seen two in my yard and the same two in the woods, so I think there are not many more than two kinds, at most—at a guess, maybe ten. But that is my great ignorance speaking. I am beginning to understand that there are dozens, if not hundreds of kinds of lichens. But perhaps now, as I begin reading the little book I bought about lichens, and become more seriously knowledgeable about them, rather than no more than idly curious, I will also be more alert to what I might see from a path in the woods, especially in winter. And by this time next year, if someone asks if I am a lichen-curious person, and, even better, engaged on a lichen-related project, I will be able to say, truthfully, that I am.

Spelling Problem

A woman from Barnard College calls me and in the course of our phone conversation she asks me if I would please spell *hemorrhaging* for her. I spell it, but wrong–maybe "hemmhoraging."

I don't like not knowing how to spell a word, since I am interested in how words are spelled.

So then I become curious and begin asking friends and others to spell that word–whenever I am talking to someone on the phone.

R. spells it "hemmorhaging."

E. spells it "hemmoraging" and then hastily changes it to "hemorhaging."

Mother spells it "hemorhaging."

Mother, before spelling it, mentions the "hae-" and "he-" choice, which E. also mentioned.

At first I think the "ae-" question is a "red herring," as I say to E. (Or a "raed haerring.") But when I try writing the word using the "ae-" form, I think maybe it isn't irrelevant after all. Maybe using the "ae-" form would make it easier to spell the rest of the word correctly.

D. spells it "hemmoraging."

S. spells it "hemhorraging."

Ann L. spells it "hemhoraging."

But all this happened fifteen years ago. And although I keep thinking back and trying to remember, I just can't remember why a woman telephoning me from Barnard College would ask me to spell the word *hemorrhaging.*

Multiple-Choice Question Posed by Stranger in Pamphlet

Question: Will suffering ever end?

Would you say:

- yes?
- no?
- maybe?

Her Selfishness

Her selfishness kept reappearing in so many different forms. She would recognize it in one form, attack it, think she knew her enemy. Then, as she was occupied with struggling against it, it would reappear in another form, or rather she would recognize it in the form of something that had been so familiar to her, so constantly there, that she had never suspected that it, too, was a form of selfishness. Oh, she would then say, so *that* is also selfishness.

Was it like a cancer?—just like! Because, as she was fighting it in one spot with all her weapons, she would recognize it in another spot. And as she was fighting it in that spot, she would see it in another. It was everywhere. But it was not like a cancer after all, because it had always been there. And she would probably not die of it.

Three Musketeers

The book *The Three Musketeers* comes in the mail. It is much larger than we expected. Early the next morning there is a strange fluffy orange cat on the fire escape looking in the window. Its eyes are wide and frightened. We think it is just a strange cat passing through. But then another cat, this one gray and fluffy, comes down the fire escape. It, too, gets onto the windowsill and looks in the window. It has lighter gray tufts sticking out of its ears and is not frightened. We think they are two young cats exploring the neighborhood. Then a third cat comes down the fire escape. It is fluffy and black. It does not get on the windowsill, but goes on down the fire escape after the others. For a while, the three cats stay in the yard. We see two of them, the gray and the black, playing together. The third, the orange one, sits at the base of a tree, we think, watching. Then we see that there is no cat sitting there, only the early sunlight shining on the orange wood

of the tree. Later, the cats are gone. Across the street, in the field, are three black cows. They have come out of the barn. Because we are new to this house, we have received gifts: three different friends have given us vases for flowers—one large, one medium, and one small. One is blue, one green, and the last mauve.

Neighbor Stare

Retired tap dancer takes his blind old poodle out of the house for a pee in the fresh snow.

At the same time, next-door neighbor, registered sex offender, who has recently moved in, leaves his rental unit by the side door.

Next-door neighbor looks up and sees tap dancer and dog.

Neighbor gives tap dancer dirty look.

Retired tap dancer sees dirty look and wonders: Why? Why is he looking at me that way?

While blind poodle pees, tap dancer ponders: Oh, probably it is only that he thinks I'm one of those rich weekenders.

Helen's Father and His Teeth

We never knew why he needed a two-pocket shirt. He smoked. This was in the old days.

So he needed one pocket for his pack of cigarettes—on the left.

But he had to have a shirt with another pocket on the right.

The answer was, it was for his teeth—he couldn't eat with his teeth in.

He would take them out at the table and slip them into his pocket. We never saw him do it.

For years, before he got his new teeth, he ate without any teeth at all. He was used to it. He could eat anything—corn on the cob!

Then he got his new teeth and he couldn't eat with them in. He tried it and he would practically choke. It would almost make him sick.

Maybe it was all in his head.

He had a lot of things in his head.

Fun

As we pick up the invitation and read it again,
the morning after,
the party still looks like fun,
even though it was not fun.

The Investigation

My fever grew worse, and I was unable to continue my investigation. But I was sure I had reached some understanding of time and history. Yet when I later read the notes I had made, I found them incoherent, marred by gaps and inconsistencies. What had seemed a revelation to me then, now seemed either obvious or not true. I was sure I had learned a few things and gained some understanding, but I was not sure if the investigation had been worthwhile. On the other hand, it was also possible that I had learned something valuable in my fever that I was not yet prepared to face in the full clarity of my recovered health.

In Truth

Whenever she wrote "in truth," an expression common to him but not to her, she thought of him, and since she had told him this, and told him also that she liked to use the phrase, as an homage to him, she knew that whenever he read the phrase as written by her he would know she had thought of him, and she suspected also that whenever he now used the expression "in truth" himself, he would also think of her.

Feeling Small

Of course, it is in some situations harder to be willing to feel small or unimportant. It is harder to be willing to feel small in relation to family members than in relation to the universe and to eternity.

It is hard to feel small and still feel strong, and good. You have to come full circle. You may start out in your life feeling small, and bad. Then you learn to feel larger, and good. Then you learn to feel smaller again, and still good.

Recurring Turnip Problem

All he had had to eat, for a while, during the war, was turnips. Now he won't eat turnips. It's the only thing he won't eat. But for years, their old friends up in Canada have misunderstood this. They think he likes turnips, maybe even loves them.

So every Thanksgiving, which the two families celebrate together, they make turnips for him. And every Thanksgiving, he eats them.

Learning to Sing

You are in a neighborhood singing group. You are singing with the others for recreation, for pleasure, not in order to perform. You enjoy it, but you are not satisfied with the way you sing. You would like to learn, at least, better control of your legato, your dynamics, your phrasing, and maybe, if you can, how to produce a better quality in your voice itself. You can read music quite easily, and you do sing on pitch, but your voice is thin and weak. One of the group suggests, after a while, that you might want to find a good singing teacher. She has a name for you.

You think it will be simple to learn to sing better. You will go to this good teacher, take lessons, and practice. She is in the next town to the north, the wife of a minister. She is very experienced and was once the coach, down in the city, to singers of opera. The lessons will take place in a room in the parsonage. You think that over time you can't help, then, but learn to sing better.

But it is not so simple. You discover during your very first lessons that the problem of singing better involves overcoming many other problems you had not ever imagined: to begin with, the problem of breathing, and the problem of how you stand—how you hold your body, how you hold your neck.

You try blowing on a candle. This is to teach you to control your breath. She has you blow steadily on the flame of a candle to see if you can make it flicker evenly. The weather is too hot to do this, it is the middle of summer, and it is, or feels like, the hottest summer you have ever experienced. But you do it. She has you expel all your breath before you inhale and sing. You should inhale as though you were sucking in the air through a straw. She asks you to watch yourself inhale in the mirror while holding your shoulders with your hands.

You are tense. You are so tense with yourself! she says. She asks you to turn your knees out and bounce, and to keep your knees slightly bent and flexible. Then she brings out a small trampoline and has you jump on it. She has you sing as you jump. This is supposed to loosen you up. She says, Yes, yes! She lends you the trampoline, you take it home, and jump up and down on it in the living room as you sing your scales.

You sing scales and practice the songs that she has assigned you. The first piece is an aria by Handel. It is a famous one, though you had not known it before. It is a beautiful aria that begins with the open syllable *La*, and the first notes are comfortably within your range. You are moved by it. But when you sing it, the sounds you make are not very pleasing to you. There on the page, as you read them, are notes that form a beautiful piece, but it is beyond your ability to create that beauty. It is your voice that is in the way. Your voice skips like the needle of a record. It squawks on some of the high notes. It is like something broken. She asks you to imagine that your voice, as it sings the melody, is a continuous golden thread.

Your teacher lends you a book on how to relax. But you are too impatient to try the exercises. You like to be active, and learning to relax is not active enough. Day after day you do not try them. You are aware of the book lying there in plain sight. Then you try one, and it seems to work. You make a good plan: you will do one exercise each day before you practice your singing. Now you begin to dread practicing and you begin to avoid it. So you drop the relaxation exercises. Some days you are pleased, when singing at least a few notes, by the sound of your voice. On other days you are very distressed, feel your heart sink, and want to cry. The unpleasant sounds are so audible, so loud, so public, even in your own living room, in privacy, in your own ears.

Your teacher recommends that you try the Alexander Technique. You make an appointment to see the teacher of the Alexander Technique, but she is very late for the appointment, too late for the lesson. You go again to see her. She says your spine has very good mobility, but that you should not consider your neck as separate from your spine. She discusses with you how you regard other people and how you regard yourself. You are so tense with yourself! says the teacher of the Alexander Technique. You are so tense with yourself! says the singing teacher again.

And why are you so critical? asks the singing teacher. Who was critical of you in your life? You think about it, but not for long. Of course, you know it was your mother. But it was your father, too—he did not disagree with your mother. It was also, sometimes, your older sister—though not your brother.

Your teacher assigns you a song by Schubert. You know the songs of Schubert very well, and many of them you like—they are satisfying in their harmonies and structures, though not moving to you. But you are holding your breath before you sing, and you shouldn't. You are taking a breath, a shallow breath, and holding it, and then singing. You should expel all the air first, take a deep breath and immediately sing, as if immediately rolling down the other side of a hill.

You are trying too hard, your teacher says. Who made you try so hard, in your life? You are assigned a song by Stefano Donaudy and then another song, one by Fauré that you have never heard before. In fact, you did not know the songs of Fauré, only the Requiem, and they become a new love. They are more moving to you than the songs by Schubert. You listen to them over and over again, as sung by Véronique Gens.

Your throat is dry, so the teacher has you take a drink of water. You take sips of water, then you burp in the middle of a scale. You can't practice without sipping water, but you can't sip water without burping. Your teacher suggests that you drink more clear fluids throughout the day and eat fresh horseradish.

Then she suggests that you see a doctor to check your nose and throat, to make sure nothing is wrong with your throat, because sometimes your voice skips.

You make an appointment. You sing more songs by Fauré. You have not forgotten to think about your tension and why you are tense. But you have one small worry: if you cease to be tense, perhaps you can't go on doing the other things in your life the way you have always done them. Do you really want to change? Do you want to relax enough to be able to sing better, but lose the tension you need to do everything else? But perhaps that won't happen.

You hope the ear, nose, and throat specialist will find something wrong, but not very wrong. It should be something simple enough for you to correct, so that then the quality of your voice will improve.

You sit in the specialist's office with a small camera up your nostril. A young resident watches your larynx and asks you to sing a note and then a higher note. The doctor who is training the young resident sings along with you. The voice problem turns out to be, possibly, not a voice problem but a stomach problem and you are given some pills to take, one each morning. You take one the next morning. Then, when you read more about the possible complications of continuing to take them, you put them away and never take another one.

The weeks are passing, and you are practicing quite regularly. You practice in the living room, standing up, always when you are alone. If someone comes into the house, by chance, they are startled by your voice, so loud in the small house, and you stop. You may be improving, very slightly. What this actually means is that most of the time, you are singing in just the same way as always, your voice thin and weak, even tremulous, but that every now and then a few notes are round and full, though not yet rich.

Your teacher tells you that you must learn to sing from your chest, specifically from your breastbone. She tells you about what she calls *apoggia*, which, she says, means leaning into the sound.

She tells you to sing sitting down, to sit back on your spine. She has you sing sitting down, with the weight of your torso on your distal—though you don't know what that means. When the singing is better, she asks you, What did you *do*? But even when you like the sound you are making, it is thin, to your ears, which to you means young.

You think what is involved is also to sing more like a woman. Maybe you have been singing like a young girl. Maybe you are in fact more like a girl than a woman. You don't know exactly what you think you are. It could also be that you think you're a boy, but it is almost certainly not that you think you're a woman. It is hard for you not to feel like a young girl, anyway, standing in front of this teacher, who is larger than you and also seems older because she is a teacher, even though in fact she is younger, though only by a few months. In the first lessons, she kept saying how small you were, though you are not someone you would ever describe as small. You are almost sure, though you don't want to ask her, that singing better also involves being more womanly, or more like a woman. You wonder if it would help to be larger. Or at least to think of yourself as larger.

The teacher of the Alexander Technique, when you see her one more time, tells you to put two pillows under your T-shirt, one in front and one in back, and practice your singing that way. The singing teacher points to a buxom statue on her piano, in order to give you the idea. It is too hot to do that, you think, it is the middle of summer, and the hottest summer in many years. You do it anyway, but there is no change in the way you sing. You remark on this to your teacher. Your teacher laughs, because you expect everything to happen right away.

She asks, another time, if you are patient. Within certain limits, you can be.

You are trying to learn to stand up straight and keep your chin down, as she has instructed. You tell her this. But not too far down, she answers. On the other hand, you keep forgetting to let your voice "drop" into your chest, into the area of your breastbone—that is, you keep forgetting about the *apoggia*, which, you remind yourself, means "leaning in."

How does she have the wisdom, you wonder, not to comment until now that you should not be singing the triplets, three against two, quite so deliberately, so correctly? You don't understand how to fix that. Then you do think you see what she means, when you listen more carefully to Véronique Gens singing the first Fauré song. You wish, yet again, that your voice were good enough so that you could concentrate, with your teacher, on musical interpretation rather than on simply producing an acceptable sound.

After some months of this, on through the fall and winter and into the spring, it is time to prepare for a recital. You are not the only one who has been studying with your singing teacher. Most of her pupils are high school students—there is only one other older woman. Some of them sing well, and there is a tenor with a truly beautiful voice. Listening to him sing, you understand what it means to be moved almost to tears just by the quality of a voice. All of her pupils will take part in the recital. You are willing—you know it is a good thing to work toward a performance. Now there is more practicing, and then there is rehearsing.

In the recital, you are to play the part of a lady attendant on the Queen of the Night, one of three attendants. That is all right with you. You like singing in harmony, which was why you joined the neighborhood singing group in the first place. Each pupil, however, is also to sing a solo, and your teacher has asked you to sing the Handel aria that you learned in your first lessons. You agree to do it, because you think that this, too, must be a good thing for your musical practice and also for your character, but you are nervous. She teaches you the small ornaments you should add when phrases are repeated, and she works out with you certain expressive hand gestures for you to use, though these seem to you rather artificial.

You would not be so nervous about simply singing the aria through accurately, from memory, if not very well. But, in addition to singing it from memory, there is another challenge. It has one rather high note that you must land on after the leap of a large interval. There is no way to make sure that you will be able to land on it successfully, without squawking. About half the time, practicing at home alone, you don't squawk when you sing it, and about half the time you do. You can guess that you will be tenser than usual up on stage, in the church, in front of the assembled audience, even though they will be mostly families and friends of the young performers. You will be alone there, except for your teacher accompanying you at the piano nearby. You will be alone with a fifty-fifty chance of emitting an embarrassing squawk. Still, you are willing to try.

The recital takes place, and as it goes along, each pupil does well. The teacher has prepared them carefully. After the piece in which you play the part of the lady attendant, you change out of your costume and into your formal clothes and stand in the wings waiting for your turn to sing the aria. You are certainly nervous, but you expected that. Then you walk out, and you sing the aria. You don't forget any of it, though you come close to forgetting. You remember the hand gestures and the ornaments. When the moment comes for you to land on the high note, you do land on it without squawking, though not with a lovely sound, and you finish singing the aria, to your great relief. After the polite applause dies down, your teacher unexpectedly addresses the audience and lets them know that you began your lessons only the previous summer and have never before sung a solo on stage in public. She is proud of you, you know. The audience applauds politely again.

After the recital, there will be a break in your lessons, since summer has come again, the high school students are away, working at their summer jobs, and you, as well as the teacher, need to rest for a little while from the intensity of the practicing and the rehearsals. A month or two later, you return to the parsonage, but now you are preparing to move away from the area, and when you do, that will be a natural end to your singing lessons. You are left with the knowledge that improving your singing ability would not be a simple matter, if you tried it again. You no longer have the illusion that by taking lessons and working diligently you could steadily improve your singing. Still, you may try again.

As for the recital, when you think back on it you still experience the same dread and nervousness, since there was never any guarantee that you would land gracefully on that note. It is true that you worked hard on the piece, and you did all you could, out there on the stage, to sing every note of the aria as you had been taught, but there was always an element of chance about your singing it successfully. You might just as well have made a dreadful squawk as you landed on the high note. That note would have been completely isolated in space, and in the attention of everyone listening, as isolated as any sound you had ever made, and it would have echoed through the vast spaces of the church, to your great embarrassment. That is why you continue to hear it in your imagination, and suffer it, though the recital is by now safely in the past.

There is a coda to this story. A few years after you move to the new place, you begin to take part occasionally in an instrumental group in which singing is optional—in other words, you may sing along to what you are playing, but you don't have to. Many people in the group don't sing because they are concentrating so hard on playing the correct chords on their instruments, most of the time bent over the frets. In the group, there is a very old woman, at least twenty years older than you. Her hands are gnarled from arthritis, so that she has to find inventive positions in which to hold and play her instrument. She is an enthusiastic and regular participant, though she usually leaves early, since she becomes tired. But it is her approach to singing that you notice. She does not have a good voice, and yet she readily volunteers to sing a favorite song to see if the group might want to learn it. You are told that she also sings in public, in front of an audience, when there is an open mic night. Her voice is thin, strained, scratchy. You don't know what to compare her high notes to—perhaps a scream of fright. But she is bold and unapologetic, with her head of curly white hair, her gleaming face, her bent back. She likes to sing these songs, and she knows a great many. And the group likes to hear her—it is her joy in the music that everyone appreciates, her good memory for lyrics, and her forceful character. You have never encountered this before—someone singing boldly and confidently with such a poor voice—and it is a surprise that gives you something to think about. You would still like to have a more pleasing voice, but you might be less afraid, now, of singing boldly and confidently, like the very old woman, with the voice that you have, such as it is.

But After All, This Is the Necessary First Stage of His Construction Work

Please, Mr. Wasp,
Stop chewing on my bench
while I'm out here trying to read!
(Or Mrs.)

Two Mayors and a Word

At a monthly meeting, the former mayor of our town stands
up and states an objection.
He is publicly upset with the current mayor.
The former mayor objects to the use of a certain word
by the current mayor:
It contains an added superfluous negative, he says,
and has no place in a town document.

The current mayor quickly concedes the point,
though with a smile whose meaning we cannot read,
and changes the document.
(The word in question is: *irregardless.*)

New Things in My Life

It takes me so long to get used to new things in my life that when I am tired I call my husband by the name of that other husband I used to have, although it was a long time ago by now, and this new son by the name of that first son I had, who was in my life for ten long years before this one came. But it is worse than that, since when I am even more tired, I remember only the other husband and the first son.

When I married that other husband I was not yet used to being a girl of eighteen but thought I was even younger, maybe twelve, and that he was my older brother, and I teased him like a little sister until he swatted me away. And then, when my first son was born, I was not yet used to being a woman of twenty-nine and thought I was younger, maybe a girl of eighteen, still a child herself, really, and not old enough to be a good mother.

Now I look at a young woman standing here before me

with her mother, and I think that her mother could be my mother too, she could be our shared mother, because I think I am still a young woman, though I am the same age as that mother. It may take me a long time to learn that I am the same age as that mother is now. But I will be still older by then, and will have learned the wrong thing.

I look at another woman of middle age, a motherly woman, and think she might be my mother, although I am nearly her age myself. But if I see that she cannot be my mother after all, I lose not only this woman, as a mother, who might have been my mother now, but also my own mother, as she was at that age.

If I continue to look at motherly women of this age, thinking they might be my mother, and wishing they might be my mother, that they might come into, or back into, my life to take care of me, I continue to forget that I am now even older than they are.

I cannot get used to the disappearance of my mother, or of my father, either, who were in charge of things and took care of things, in their own way, and who took care of me, and of all of us, who made plans and changed them, who lost their way in the car and found it again, who lost their keys to the house, to the car, and to the hotel room, and found them again. I cannot get used to the disappearance of that beautiful older sister pursued by neatly dressed college men, or to the disappearance of that high school student older brother with his Latin grammar and his touch-typing manual and his cello.

Sometimes I forget I am a woman at all, and at these times I am not inside this woman's body with its many signs of age, but inside a smaller body, a body half this size, a body with no gender, or not much, a body that only wants to go out into the sunlit backyard and climb the apple tree.

Not Much to Tell

David writes me a note, delivered by Carol. He tells me, in the note, about a woman in a supermarket recycling center trying to redeem shampoo bottles for money. He thinks I'll be interested. I am.

I ask, by email, Please tell me more.

He answers, by email, Oh, that's all there is. There isn't anything else.

I ask, When was it? Where? How many bottles? Why did she do this? What did other people do?

He gives in and sends me another note, subject line: "Not much to tell." It reads:

Time—early morning, after breakfast, when geezers like to shop.

Place—narrow hallway in Watertown Price Chopper's bottle return, sticky floors, stale beer smell.

Character—woman in her fifties holding a plastic bag of

recycles, trying to get a nickel for a shampoo bottle. She's having no luck, but she's not frustrated and tries other bottles. At last, a man near her leans over, whispers, and she stops.

Late Afternoon

How long the shadow is,
coming across the counter,
from this grain of salt.

Worrying About Father's Arm

How will we solve the problem of how Father sleeps on his right arm? He is not comfortable, his arm is under him, it hurts him as it presses into his ribs, and it is hurt by the weight of his body pressing down on it. He tells us this, with a gentle smile, as though to say it is not important, and not our problem.

Father died many years ago. But the problem is still there on my mind, unresolved, even though Father no longer tries to sleep comfortably and in fact no longer has an arm.

Opportunistic Seed

She holds the door for him as he carries a case of wine into
the house.
A seed floating in its bit of fluff takes the opportunity to
enter the house behind him
(though this will turn out to be, for the seed, not a good
move).

Our Young Neighbor and His Little Blue Car

Our young neighbor and his noisy little blue car: how he tears up and down the roads around here very early in the morning. He is not really going anywhere, and he is not testing his engine, as he sometimes does in his backyard. Before dawn, he races past our house and down to the end of our road, and turns north onto the main road past the deli. We hear the sound of his engine becoming fainter and fainter and vanishing. Surely it wakes or rouses everyone along his route. After he has been away for ten minutes, he turns around and heads home. We hear his engine again, at first faint amid the silence, then growing louder and louder, until it is upon us. It must be that, miles away, he thought of us, afraid that we had gone gratefully back to sleep, wishing to rouse us again. But once he has been home for a little while, he must think of the many houses on the main road, where some people, surely, have also gone gratefully back to sleep, and he must feel it is time to take his car out onto our road again, down to the end of it, and up the main road again past the deli. And then, after a short time, several miles away, it must be that he remembers our road again, with its peaceful hayfields, its meadows and woods, its front yards in the brightening dawn, the dew just beginning to shine on the grass, and he feels impelled to return, to bring some life to us, and so he heads back, and once more we hear his engine, at first faint amid the silence, then growing louder and louder, until it is upon us.

Or perhaps he is merely our town crier, making his rounds. All is well!

Those Two Loud Women

Those two loud women–
if they're going to talk so constantly near me on the train,
they could *at least* have an interesting conversation,
one that I would like to overhear!

Winter Letter

Dear Kids,

I'll try not to let this go on forever, because Dad gets restless if I'm busy at something for too long. So I'll just tell you some of what we've been up to.

It has been really cold, with a lot of snow, so we've been indoors a lot. We're trying to eat healthy, and our best new discovery is, guess what . . . radishes! Dad brings them home from the store every week. They come in all different colors, and I even cook the radish greens. Another thing is, I'm making my own applesauce now. We were buying it in jars, but then one day I read the label and what do you think I discovered? The apples are grown clear up in Canada, and then they're shipped to California, the applesauce is made in Santa Cruz, California, and then it's shipped back East. And here we are right in the middle of apple country! So now I make my own.

Then I started reading the labels of all the food we get. Can you believe the vegetable bouillon cubes I like so much come from Switzerland! And the breadcrumbs Dad likes best are made in Japan. Breadcrumbs!—that's just plain embarrassing.

So I'm making more of our food from scratch. I'm also sitting in a different chair at the kitchen table. I had to move once because one of the cats was on my chair, and I discovered that I liked looking at the trees out the window instead of at the shelves of dishes. So we're going to try that.

I know this isn't too fascinating, but it's our life.

A note about the wild creatures here—inside the house! There are so many ladybugs in the kitchen. One will drop down onto the counter. I never know if it's the same one. I like to watch what they do, how they walk around on their little legs. I looked them up in our bug book, and it said they only eat aphids, but that's not true. I've tried them on marmalade, cat food, lettuce, and celery. They like them all. I like to watch the way they turn over, when they end up on their back. First they wave their legs in the air and try to catch hold of something, and when that doesn't work, they open their wings out to the sides and kind of flip themselves over.

I try to go outdoors every day for at least a little while, no matter how cold it is. It's a little boring in the yard, but I walk all the way around it a couple of times. I study the animal tracks in the snow. Usually all I see are rabbit tracks, but once I saw possum tracks going along by the barn. At least I thought they might be possum, and when I got inside and looked them up, I was right. Their little toes point out in all directions like stars.

I wanted to collect some birds' nests, which you can find more easily in winter, but your dad said they might smell, or carry a disease, like avian flu.

We do have our frustrations. Dad still can't find that nice little wine-colored cloth bag you gave him for Christmas, his favorite, which he always took to get the mail. I tell him there are plenty of others, but he wants that one. And the cats—sometimes we find a puddle on the floor in the morning, or some spit-up, or they've unrolled the toilet paper onto the floor.

We're together all day long, which can be hard. We disagree about things, like which kitty litter to use, or when to have dinner. Sometimes I try to work on our relationship—i.e., be nicer—but your dad is always more or less the same, winter or summer, nice except when he's in a bad mood. Then he'll accuse me of things, like, did I try to move the shower head?

One thing I'm looking forward to is an outing we're going on in a few days, to the local library. Your dad is always pretty cheerful when we're out of the house, though it's true that the farther away we go, the more cheerful he gets, and we're not going that far.

Speaking of outings, you wanted to hear more about our trip to the Texas hill country back in October. I'll tell you now, before I forget completely. You knew we went, and that we got a lot of rain while we were there, but I didn't tell you the whole story.

As you know, we went down there to spend a couple of days looking at the vegetation and to see my friend Bea and her new house and her dog (and her husband). Well, the trip down was okay. We shared a sandwich and some chips on the airplane, then we both looked at our airplane magazines—Dad likes to open up the foldout map and find where we are—and then Dad did his Sudoku puzzles while I read my Michael Crichton book (and fell asleep, Dad told me later, sitting bolt upright with my finger keeping my place in the book!).

Bea picked us up at the airport and drove us right to

her house. Our plan was to spend the first evening with her, then stay at the inn the next day, because Bea was busy. Then we would spend the following day with Bea again. It didn't work out that way.

We had fun looking through Bea's house and playing with her cute little dog Henry. Henry has a trick where Bea wraps his toy tight in a towel and tosses it on the floor and Henry unwraps the towel and finds the toy. Their house is in a nice neighborhood and cost them a lot of money, she said, because everybody is moving to Austin now. They had to take out two mortgages. I can imagine. We hadn't met her husband before, and we sat in their living room and talked to him for a while. He seemed nice. He has a desk where he works standing up! Then Bea and I went out to eat at a Japanese restaurant. Your dad and her husband had started talking about something interesting, so they decided just to stay home and have a couple of beers and make themselves a sandwich (American-style!). At the Japanese restaurant, the waiters bring out all these courses which the chef chooses for you, in tiny portions. Bea's eating this kind of food now. It certainly was interesting.

Then Bea drove us out to the inn, which she had trouble finding in the dark—and boy, was it dark. The inn is at the end of a long winding road through ranch land. We were ready for bed by then. But we didn't sleep all that well because the bed was very, very soft, with one of those pillow-top inserts under the bottom sheet, and also the quilt was very heavy. I get the feeling people in Texas use air-conditioning all the time, no matter what the temperature is outside, so then they have to sleep under all this heavy bedding.

Well, we like to sleep on a firm mattress with no quilt and the window open. So the next morning I completely remade the bed. Dad couldn't watch—you know how he hates it when I get fanatical. So he went for a little walk around the place. When I was done, he took me out and showed me what he had discovered—a huge vegetable garden they have there, next to the driveway. I was impressed.

The inn is really nice. It consists of a few two-storied wooden buildings with open balconies front and back. (Our room was on the second floor.) It's up on top of a hill with a lot of acreage around it—something like 80 acres, which of course isn't considered a lot in Texas. We learned while we were there that even 4,000 acres wasn't considered much in Texas in the old days. But times have changed.

We knew they gave tours of the ranch, and we had signed up for one, since this was our day by ourselves. It's really a tour of the hill country itself—the plants and animals, etc. It takes two hours. What it is, is they take you in a jeep, very slowly, around the different parts of the ranch, some distance away from the main buildings. Every now and then they stop the jeep so you can get out and stretch your legs and look at things a little more closely. They tell you whatever you want to know, but they don't talk too much, which is nice. (I asked a lot of questions, of course.) I sat up front with the driver, who was actually the owner of the place, and Dad sat in the back seat with a couple of the other guests as well as a young employee of the inn who came along to open the gates. Some of the ground we drove over was pretty bumpy and we had to hold on tight not to get knocked around—quite an experience, with a lot of jiggling!

We set off at ten. First we drove down by the creek to look at where the flooding was last spring—it really took out a lot of trees. There was a dead tree lying on its side there, and it was full of buzzards. The driver (owner), Pete, said that before the flood, the birds used to perch up in these same trees, when they (the trees) were alive and standing up. We got out and walked down toward the water. The birds flew up and circled overhead for a while, then landed in another tree farther away. There were two kinds of buzzards, almost the same, but when they're in the air you can see a different pattern on their wings. Pete told us more about the flood and the river itself, and then we got back in the jeep and went on.

We drove through areas where goats and cattle were grazing, and horses. We had to keep stopping so this young man, Jeffrey or Jeremy, could open the gates and close them behind us. He was very nice, and energetic. The main vegetation there was live oak trees and lots and lots of prickly pear cactus, which is an odd combination, I think.

We stopped again high up, at a lookout platform with a view down to the river. There was a Texas flag flying from the railing—a little the worse for wear, I have to say. Then we stopped at the very highest point of the property, where they had built a little cabin you could rent for a weekend—if you didn't mind having no electricity and using an outhouse!

Actually, that got me started talking to Pete about composting toilets. I've actually used one. They are so quiet, and they don't smell at all. I thought the inn should install some, especially given that drought and water shortages might become a problem. But Pete didn't seem very interested, and I knew that although your dad was probably smiling politely, there in the back seat, he wasn't enjoying this conversation.

Then he interrupted me to ask Pete a question about the design of the Texas flag. I got the message and stopping talking about toilets.

Toward the end of the tour, we were lucky enough to see a roadrunner cross the track right in front of us, almost under the jeep. Actually, I was the only one who saw it (besides the driver). I've never seen one before. They're dark brown, and not very big, with long straight tails sticking out in back of them. I looked them up later—there was a bird book in our room—and it's really true that they don't fly, they only run. We also saw a whole cloud of little yellow butterflies once, in front of us, or they could have been white. They were feeding on coyote dung, Pete said. We got back to the inn around noon.

The rest of the day was more relaxing. After lunch we explored the inn itself—they have a little library with some shelves of military history that interested Dad—and then we looked at the brochures and other things in our room. Then we lay down and read for a while and napped. Dinner was great—the place has the best restaurant for miles around, apparently—and after dinner we talked to some of the other guests out on the back porch. They were pretty friendly. We had thought there would be people from all over the country visiting the Texas hill country, but most of these people seemed to be from Houston. They really do have a different accent down in Texas. Instead of "sleep" they say "slape." Instead of "green" they say "grane." Dad made friends with a man from Houston who's also interested in military history. We went to bed early–it had already been a pretty active couple of days!

Our plan with Bea was for her to pick us up after breakfast the next day (her husband was busy, she said). She was going to take us to see the one tourist attraction near here, in the closest town, and that's the house Katherine Anne Porter used to live in. Actually, she didn't live in it very long, and it belonged to her grandmother. But she's the famous person around here–our room at the inn was even called the Porter Room.

But–guess what? Nature had other ideas. In the middle of the night we were woken up by a loud thunderstorm. In fact it was a really violent storm, with thunder and lightning and rain pounding on the balcony outside our door. The balcony is wide open to the elements. Out our window, we could see the whole sky with the flashes of lightning. The rain went on and on.

Then, the next morning, at eight o'clock, we got a call

from the front desk. They said there was a tornado warning, and all the guests were asked to come downstairs to the kitchen. We were still in our pajamas. They said there was a danger of a tornado for the next half hour, then it would be over. So I didn't think we should take the time to get dressed. Your dad didn't care as much about the tornado as about appearing in his pajamas, so he put on some clothes, but I went out in the terry-cloth robe provided by the inn. We went down by the balcony stairs because it was quicker. The rain was coming at us sideways, against the side of the building, and the wooden deck of the balcony was slippery, and so were the steps, so we had quite a time even getting down there without falling. I had brought along my little folding umbrella from Paris, but the wind was blowing so hard I didn't put it up.

Of course I was the only one in a bathrobe. And I make a pretty large object in a white terry-cloth robe, especially in a fairly small room, which the breakfast room was. But you know me—I'm at an age where I just don't get embarrassed by things like that. The room was cheerful, no one seemed afraid of the tornado, though of course everyone was talking about the weather, and people were coming in soaking wet and laughing, carrying towels. We helped ourselves to mugs of coffee from the urn and sat down and waited for the warning to be over. We chatted a little with some of the other guests. We didn't really expect a tornado, and we didn't get one.

But the rain just went on and on, and we were told later, after breakfast, that it had rained so hard during the night that the water was rising in a lot of the creeks and rivers around us, and even covering some of the roads. Then I have to say we got a little nervous, though the inn is on high ground. A young couple who were supposed to leave that day decided to chance it, and we heard them talking about which way to try and get out.

Then we got news that the roads were completely flooded and in fact the whole town had shut down. Everyone was supposed to stay in their houses. We talked to Bea on my phone and canceled our plans with her.

I'm not sure your dad was sorry. I think he was happier staying at the inn, which was really pleasant and had great food and some good books, than going touring around with a pair of women who might talk his ears off. I wasn't all that interested, myself, but I wanted to see Bea. Anyway, though your Dad and I are such readers, we haven't read anything by Katherine Anne Porter, though we know the name of her most famous book—*The Ship of Fools*. Which I bet you two don't, being too young—have you ever even heard of it? In fact, there was a copy of it on the mantelpiece in our room. (We had our own fireplace, and, if you can believe it, the fireplace went right through to the bathroom, so you could have a fire in there, too, if you wanted.) I opened it and looked at the beginning and saw there was a "cast of characters" that went on for three pages! Right away I knew I'd never read that novel. Still, I like old houses and I always enjoy taking a tour of a historic place. And I was sorry I wouldn't get to spend some more time with Bea. That was one of the reasons we came down. We were flying home the next day. So that first evening with Bea and her husband and her little dog Henry was it.

Well, later on, after lunch, we had a clear spell. The clouds seemed to break up a little. The sky was still stormy looking, but brighter. After we played cards for a while, your dad lay down to read a book he had picked out of the library downstairs, about Julius Caesar, and I decided to go for a walk. Here was my big adventure! I always like going out on my own for a while, when we're traveling. I walk more slowly than your dad. He likes to get where he's going. I like to take my time and look at everything a lot longer than he does.

Anyway, he said he had had enough of a walk already, going out to see the vegetable garden.

I thought I'd head for the river. It's called Onion Creek. I didn't ask why. It's quite far down below where the inn is—you could see part of it through the trees from the back balcony on the second floor. I had gone out there earlier in the day and looked at it through the bird-watching binoculars they had in the room. I thought I saw logs and other debris being carried downstream. I thought from the dramatic reports that morning that maybe I'd see a shed or an animal floating down, but I didn't.

First I went and got a laminated folding map from the office. They also had walking sticks in a barrel by the path, near the back porch. So I took a stick. I had walking shoes on, but they're really for city walking, so they turned out not to be terribly good on this path, which was very rocky and still wet from the rain—slippery and muddy. The laminated map showed the different trails and also had numbers that matched numbers next to trees and shrubs along the path identifying different plants and giving information about them, such as what the Native Americans used them for. This was interesting, though I couldn't always find the numbers and I got a little tired trying to remember the facts about each plant. It just seemed that some part of every plant was used by the Native Americans for medicinal purposes.

Anyway, I had the strangest experience almost right away, when I had been walking only about ten minutes. I had passed a few different numbers and stopped to read about the plants. Then the path started sloping down a little, and I came to a sort of crossroads, where another path crossed my path. I stopped to look for it on the map. On the map it was yellow. Then I looked up and to the left, along the other path, and I was very startled to see a kind of gray face looking at me. It wasn't very high up off the ground, and I realized after a second that it was the face of a raccoon. He was about twenty feet away, sitting or squatting straight up facing me. The face just sort of floated there about the leaves—I couldn't see the rest of his body because of a curve in the path (his path).

After I saw him, I didn't move. He stayed still, too. Then he went back down on all fours and very calmly went into the long grass on one side of his path, with his nose to the ground, and then came out again and nosed a little in the grass on the other side of his path. Then he returned to his path and started coming toward me. His head was down and he was sniffing and nosing along the path as he came, paying no attention to me. I wondered if he knew I was there. He kept coming toward me with a sort of waddling motion. Now I was just a little frightened. I had never had a wild animal come walking toward me before. He didn't seem rabid, but I remembered hearing something about that–if wild animals came near you in daylight they might be rabid.

I thought surely he must smell me. Then he straightened up again, squatting on his hind legs, and he did seem to be sniffing the air. His face was directed toward me and his nose was up. I thought now he would get alarmed and turn and run. But he just put his nose back down to the path and came waddling on forward, closer and closer, looking at the ground. He went off into the grass a couple more times, sniffed around and pawed the ground, then came out again. Finally, he was only a few feet away–I could almost touch him. Now I really was afraid. I thought that at any moment he would see that I was there, and then he might leap right at me and bite me. But I still didn't move–I wanted to see what would happen. I could see his face clearly. One of his eyes was milky white. Then I thought maybe he had a cataract in it, and couldn't see out of it. In fact, maybe he couldn't see well at all. Maybe he was old, though he looked pretty healthy. His fur was a little matted down in places. Maybe he was old and couldn't see or smell very well.

He didn't seem to know I was there. He stopped and stood still on his four paws, but he didn't look in my direction. Then he went on across my path, and onto the other side of his path, and finally in among the shrubbery, and disappeared. I stayed there another minute, but he didn't reappear.

What was most strange about this experience was that I felt invisible, or more than that—I felt as though I weren't there at all. I don't know how to describe it. Surely, if a wild animal could walk past right in front of you and not notice you at all, you weren't really there.

When I talked to some people about it later, they said, Well, maybe he was used to people because of the inn. But I don't think animals just ignore you like that. They run away or they attack you or they beg for food. Don't you think so? I could have been a tree.

Well, after that, I was nervous. I thought I might meet up with another wild animal, like a coyote. The ranch owner, Pete, had said there were no bears around, but there were lots of coyotes. He kept Great Pyrenees dogs in the pastures with his goats because of the coyotes. I decided to go on with my walk anyway. After all, even though I had had a little adventure, I hadn't gotten very far—I could still see the inn behind me.

I followed the path to a bench and a view of the creek down below. The water was pretty high, and a light brown color, but, strangely, now it was flowing in the opposite direction. Of course that couldn't have been true. I must have got it wrong that morning, even though I had looked carefully through the binoculars. I kept on walking. Now the path sloped down toward the water. But the clouds had gathered again, and they were darker, and a few raindrops began to fall. The path got steeper and steeper, and my city shoes were slipping and sliding—I was glad I had taken the walking stick. But I was afraid that if I went all the way down to the creek, I would have a terrible time getting back up. I was also afraid the rain would come down really hard again. And the water might rise so fast that I would be pulled in and swept away.

So when I came to another path that led back up to the inn—it was red on the map—I took it. I hadn't had much of a walk, but I felt immediately better heading back to safety. And it did start raining hard again just then. I was pretty wet by the time I got near the inn.

On the back porch, the manager was showing a new guest the path and the barrel of walking sticks. She was telling her about the laminated maps. The guest was smiling, and she smiled at me, too, as I came up to the porch. But I'm not sure I was a very good advertisement for the inn, with my wet clothes and muddy shoes, struggling along through the rain and probably still looking a little frightened.

I won't bore you with the rest—how I asked for a rag to clean my shoes and they brought me a huge old towel, how awkward it was to clean off the mud with that old towel at a hose by the garden shed, balancing on one foot, etc. (And it was still raining.) But when some of the mud was off, I went back up to the room and cleaned the shoes some more in the bathroom, and then told Dad about my adventure with the raccoon, though I don't think he really understood how strange it was. He was in the middle of something interesting in his book and wanted to get back to his reading.

So, anyway, that was more or less it—our only real vacation in a while. The next morning, of course, was bright and sunny. It would have been perfect weather for meeting Bea and touring the Katherine Anne Porter house. But off we went to the airport—the same nice young man drove us who had opened all those gates on the tour—and we were early enough so I could pick up some Texas-themed items in the gift shop, mainly Christmas presents for my book club. We did almost the same things on the flight back as on the flight down—sandwich, chips, Michael Crichton, nap—except that your dad, instead of doing Sudoku, sat and thought about Julius Caesar. I could tell, because now and then he'd share some fact with me, like that Caesar's army could build a bridge across a river in one day, or that if an enemy was hiding in a forest they would cut down the whole forest (!), or that they mainly ate bread. We like flying, I have to say.

So we had fun, though it was kind of a strange trip, all in all. We had thought we wouldn't like Texas, for all the reasons you can guess. But that hill country is beautiful. And the people were nice. After we were back a few days, Bea sent us a bag of pecans from the tree in Katherine Anne Porter's yard! They taste good though they're hard to get out of the shell.

Just a couple of last things—one is about that outing we have planned. It's not as far away as Texas! Dad isn't enthusiastic, but he's being a good sport about it. What it is, they're having an Apron Exhibit at the library. It's this one woman's collection of colorful old aprons, and they have invited people to bring their own apron to display, too. So I may look in a couple of drawers and see what I have, though most of mine are stained. They're also going to teach an apron-making class, but I don't really want to make an apron.

Another thing I saw in our local paper is a series of classes on foot massage. It turns out, they say–which I didn't know–that the soles of our feet have a map of our entire body. Each part of our foot corresponds to a different part of our body. The article says the woman teaches you how to knead, rub, rock, and shake your feet. Of course your dad wouldn't want anyone showing him how to rub and shake his feet, but I'm interested.

Well, you wanted a long letter, handwritten like in the old days, and you got it. How is your life in the city?? We miss you. You haven't visited in a while.

We've been cooped up inside all day, it's not too cold, and we need to get out and stretch our legs. I think we'll probably take this letter down to the post office and also see if they have any new stamps. Sometimes we buy a couple of sheets of stamps that we like. Then, back at home, we have a cup of tea and turn over the sheets and read the descriptions on the other side–they're often quite informative.

Love to you both, and from Dad,
Mother

Caruso

He often wondered, when he was a child, why his father would sit there crying as he listened to a phonograph record of Enrico Caruso singing.

Later, when he was a grown man, he and his father would sit there together, crying as they listened to Caruso.

Pearl and Pearline

We knew this lady named Pearl. She lived down the road from us. She was sort of a friend of the family. Pearl used to clean the house by shoving everything under the sofa and behind the sofa, and under the chairs and into the closets. So, in our family, whenever we had to clean up the house in a hurry for visitors, we said we were cleaning it "the Pearl way."

Pearl and Fred weren't able to have children, so they adopted a little girl. She was a pretty little thing. Her name was Michelle. Pearl wasn't very nice to her, the rumor was. Pearl was what we called a wet-brain—she drank a lot. They both drank a lot. They lived out in the woods—no one could hear them if they started shouting. They ended up in the state prison and the state hospital for rehab, a couple of times. I had to drive one of them to court—every month for eight months! I had to take my kid along with me because I couldn't leave her home. The judge complained because we had food in the courtroom. What else was I going to do?

I got along with them, but I was always walking on eggshells. How did Michelle turn out? She turned out okay. She grew up and joined the Navy.

As for whatever happened to Pearl, she left Fred, in the end. And guess what she did? She went off somewhere to become a belly dancer! After she left, of course Fred needed a housekeeper. He found one, and what do you think her name was? Pearline! That was before he got married again.

What You Could Get for Your Turnips

During the month of October in 1852, 1853, and the following years, George Holcomb's turnip harvest was at its height. With his family and hired help, sometimes three Irishwomen, he would pull and cut turnips on many days in succession, sometimes topping them and sometimes leaving the tops on. After the turnips were harvested, he would trade them, even into the new year, for goods and services including:

Half a bushel of turnips to Henry Cranston's store for a pound of ginger.
Two bushels of turnips to the shoemaker Tyler Ayers for 50 cents on account toward mending shoes.
One bushel of turnips to Henry Platt for 25 cents in cash.
Five bushels of turnips to Mr. Mason for a pair of boots for daughter Sarah.
Two bushels of turnips to George Clark for 25 cents each.

Three bushels to Benjamin Lord, value 75 cents, in exchange for the following goods at Charles Wheeler's store: one yard cotton velvet for a vest, 40 cents, one dozen buttons, 6 cents, two pencils, 2 cents, and three pounds of sugar, 27 cents.

An unspecified quantity of turnips to the tailor Jervins for the cutting of a coat and vest for son John.

One bushel of turnips for credit amounting to 25 cents with blacksmith Walker and one bushel for same with blacksmith Stone, and half a bushel for credit amounting to 12½ cents with Doctor Bates.

Sixty-eight cents' worth of turnips to Lias Dike in exchange for him chopping George's sausage meat.

Two bushels of turnips to Manuel Buten for his help in pulling turnips.

Two and a half bushels to J. Acox for a new beam on son George's side hill plow, which son John broke.

Three bushels of turnips to the Irishman shoemaker who lives in the Clark house, one bushel paid for and the other two owing 50 cents.

Turnips worth 87 cents to Peases Harness Shop for a leather cover whip and buckskin lash, on trust.

To Asa Palmer, three and a half bushels that was on a contract for shoeing a horse which pays him up.

To George P. Glass factory and his workmen, six bushels of turnips, paid for in red flannel at 25 cents per yard. With bargain to carry him and his workmen more turnips and again take his pay in flannel.

Five bushels of turnips to Wm. L. Brown's store for two gallons of molasses and five and a half pounds of sugar.

Six bushels of turnips to Lias Dike at 25 cents per, for the same credited in tallow.

An unspecified quantity of turnips to be paid to an Irishman that lives in Wm. B. Maxon's house hired by son George to pull the wool from three dead sheep.

Half a bushel of turnips to Henry Lapum to pay in full for a previously acquired barn shovel.

A Woman Offering Magazines

I have been quarreling on the phone with a woman who in the end did not seem like a real woman, or even a real human being. I gave her a small bit of my humanity and she annihilated it suddenly, in a lightning bolt. This was disturbing to me not because she was angry when she hung up on me, but because she was not angry. She hung up suddenly only because I was no longer useful to her.

In fact, we did not really quarrel. And, really, there was no "we." But the conversation was certainly on the phone. She did hang up on me, and it is fair to say "she," even though by then she did not seem like a real woman, to my way of thinking.

She wanted to offer me an immense number of magazines. She was offering five different magazines, sixty copies of one, one hundred twenty of another, and so on, and also a free camera. She said she wasn't selling anything. And she seemed, briefly, to share with me the idea that there had to be a catch to the offer somewhere, but there wasn't. She seemed to talk to me and hear my answers, though there was sometimes a strange intonation in her voice. Then she asked me suddenly, with frightening specificity, if I already subscribed to five magazines. I said I did. And then she had no more use for me and hung up.

Marriage Moment of Annoyance—Dinner

They have been discussing what to have for dinner.
Finally, he says she can be the one to decide what to cook.
He watches her begin to prepare their food and adds, with a frown,
"Nothing that's going to make me sick, though . . ."

Marriage Moment of Annoyance—Speculations

He says:
No, I *don't* care
about your speculations
as to what was there
before the universe existed.

Unhappy Christmas Tree

An old woman believes that her Christmas tree wants to get married.

Her caretaker says:

—No, it's just a tree. See? Come here! Feel it!

The old woman feels a branch.

—Oh, you're right, it is a tree.

But the old woman is still worried.

—But inside . . . inside, there is a woman who wants to come out and get married.

The old woman will not be convinced she is wrong. She sits for an hour staring at the tree.

After an hour, the caretaker says:

—Come on, don't worry. It's only a tree.

—But it's so sad, it's so sad for her . . . With those little things all over her . . . Are they little men?

—No, don't worry, they're not little men. Those are your ornaments. You've had them for years. Every year we take them out and hang them on the tree.

—But they're hurting her! They're pinching her! She just wants to come out and get married.

Improving My German

All my life I have been trying to improve my German.
At last my German is better!
But now I am old and ill.
I will die soon.
But when they take me to my grave,
I will have,
somewhere in my brain,
better German.

V

Poem of Greeting

Hello My Dear,
how are you
i hope fine
i am janet by name
a lady

i will like you to reply me
about my relationship
with you
i will tell you more about me
Greeting from,
Janet

Two Stories About Boys

My friend Tom tells me a story. He has lived in the same house since he was a child. Until about a decade ago, he lived there with his mother, then she died and he went on living there alone. Neither when his mother was alive nor afterward was the house altered very much from what it had been in his childhood. Recently, he decided to make some changes in his bathroom, and part of the work involved removing the "surround" of the bathtub. When the builder began to tear it away, he discovered something: stacked neatly by one foot of the tub were half a dozen very old cans of tuna fish, unopened, rusted.

For a time, this was a mystery. Tom thought and thought about these cans of tuna fish that had been stacked there by the hidden clawfoot of his bathtub for so long. Then at last he remembered: some sixty-odd years ago, when he was a child, he and his friends were told more than once by the grown-ups, who watched the news every night, about the imminent danger of nuclear war. The boys were little by little instilled with a fear of this catastrophe. As a precaution, Tom's closest friend, an enterprising boy, took the cans of tuna fish, one by one over time, so as not to be found out, from his family's kitchen cupboard and secreted them inside the tub surround at Tom's house, as an emergency provision in case of nuclear war.

I thought of this story when I was out in the Midwest, in Iowa City. I was walking through a historic old mansion that was now the home of a large and prosperous interior design business. I was visiting this house because it had been well known to my mother in her childhood. I was wandering upstairs and down, in and out of the rooms, former bedrooms that now contained bolts of cloth and wallpaper books, because my mother had told me many stories about it from when she was very young. It had been the home of a cousin of hers, a wealthy girl—unlike my mother, who was poor. My mother had visited her cousin there many times—the girls were close friends. I have a photograph of my mother as a little girl standing with her mother, who is dressed all in black, with this house in the background. After many years had passed, the heirs of the cousin's family had sold the house and it had been converted into an orphanage.

I fell into conversation with the owner of the interior design firm, telling him about my mother and her cousin. He listened attentively and then in turn told me a story. During the time in which the house was used as an orphanage, the curving, broad oak banister that ran two flights up through the generous stairwell of the house had been freshly painted. One of the orphans, a boy of nine or ten, in a fit of mischievousness, had stood at the top of the stairs and cut open a feather pillow above the freshly painted banister. The feathers had floated down and stuck to the paint.

The years passed, and the place changed hands several times, the banister being repainted from time to time. Finally, the mansion came into the possession of the design firm, which embarked on a thorough renovation. The banister was to be sanded down to its original wood, and for this the firm hired a local man. He took layer after layer of the old paint off the wood until he came to the layer in which he could detect the remains of those same feathers, dried into the old paint. He knew what they were. He was the same boy who, living there as an orphan, had cut open the pillow and scattered the feathers.

Claim to Fame #5: Rex Dolmith

In Taos, New Mexico, in 1949, my parents in their rental apartment were bothered by the constant noise from the tenants in the apartment above them. Their upstairs neighbors were, it turns out, the Taos painter Rex Dolmith and his family!

Unfinished Business

Cleaning up, in the kitchen, she goes to wipe away a small black seed from the counter.

But the small black seed moves, and then walks hastily off in the other direction.

No, I am not a seed, the little bug seems to be saying.

No, it is not saying anything, but going off on its own, reminded by her sponge that it has business elsewhere.

Lost by Yanda Hedge (Personal)

round eyeglasses
faux tortoiseshell
somewhere
between nursery school
and sacred space,
possibly
covered by snow.

After Reading Peter Bichsel

Last spring and summer, I was reading the stories of the Swiss writer Peter Bichsel. I began reading them in Vienna. The little book—a hardcover, but small and light-weight—was a gift from a German friend at the start of my trip, to provide me with something to read in German, since I wanted to improve my facility in the language. I had brought with me from home a paperback thriller by a very popular German writer, but I wasn't enjoying it: the plot, so far, was tiresome, the main character unpleasant, and the tone sarcastic. My friend thought she could find something better for me, and she was right. I continued reading Bichsel's stories on the train from Vienna to Salzburg, and then in Salzburg, and then on the train to Zurich, and then in Zurich, Berlin, Hamburg, Cologne, and on each train I took to go from one city to the next.

In fact, Peter Bichsel regularly writes about reading and about train journeys. He will also sometimes begin a story, or remark in the middle of a story, "There are stories that are hardly worth telling," or "There is almost nothing to say about X", and then sometimes follow that with a "but": "But I have wanted to tell this story for a long time now," or "But it has to be told, because it was the first story in my life, the first one that I remember." He then goes on to tell a lovely, quiet, modest story, a story that glows with human kindness, or love, or some combination of compassion, understanding, and honesty. (Or am I, these days, finding this quality so marked in his stories because I am seeking it?)

I was reading his stories as I traveled, but I was also distracted by all that I saw and experienced, so I did not often think about his stories when I was not reading them. But then I particularly thought of him and his stories after an experience I had in Salzburg. I wanted to describe this experience, but I wanted to say, near the beginning of my story, that there was not much to tell, because, really, so little happened: there was a scene, one that involved a peculiar character, and later a coincidence.

I had stopped for lunch at a small, undistinguished restaurant that I had picked out earlier in the day, on my way through the town and across the river to find Mozart's birthplace. It looked to me like a reliable sort of local place, without pretensions, not expensive, not particularly attractive to tourists, but frequented by locals. Its entrance was set back from the main street and it was called Café Central. Rain was falling in the street outside, and the umbrella stand inside the door was filled with wet umbrellas. The coat tree was hung with damp jackets and slickers. The colors of the place were strikingly tan, brown, and cream. The first part of the room, where one entered, contained the bar and was partitioned off from the main room to serve bar customers at small tables. A shelf along the top of the partition held stacks of folded newspapers and magazines for the customers.

The place was quite crowded, though not yet entirely full, and noisy, since this was the height of the lunch hour. A buxom, energetic woman who seemed to be the manager or co-owner of the place showed me to a cramped spot in a line of little tables against one wall, but after she went away, and after a moment's hesitation, I got up and walked on back to look for a more comfortable spot. I found a roomier and more peaceful seat in the far corner, at a small table between two tables already occupied. To my left was a large corner table surrounded by banquettes, and to my right, a small table for two, identical to my own.

At the large table were seated a man and a woman, evidently a couple, though for a long time they did not speak to each other. The man was calmly and very thoroughly reading a newspaper, and the woman was sitting completely still beside him and gazing off into the distance with a placid and agreeable expression on her face. I am left with the impression, now, that the man was Asian, though I can't be sure of this. The woman was not. Try as I may, to retrieve a more exact image of the man's face, there is no more memory available to me and I cannot do it. It is not relevant to the story, anyway, but this vague impression adds to my sense of the difference or disparity between the two of them, though they seemed comfortable and companionable.

It was the woman at the table to my right who came to interest me the most during that lunch hour, although at first, in my preoccupation with settling into my seat, putting my bags down beside me, bringing out something to read, and looking around to take in the sights and sounds of the room, I did not pay particular attention to her. It was only as I became used to my surroundings, having examined the features of the room, the customers in my part of it—the larger part—and those beyond the partition, having absorbed the sights and sounds of this place and taken note of any more unusual elements or occupants, that my attention was more and more drawn to my neighbor.

I had ample time to observe her, as well as the others in the restaurant, because, although the young waitress and the older manager both kept rushing back and forth without a pause among the tables, taking orders and carrying food, my order was very long in coming—thirty minutes, forty minutes. Since I was tired from my morning of wandering through the streets of the older parts of Salzburg on this side of the river and across the bridge on the other side, stopping to read plaques and look into shop windows, crossing back over the long bridge, I did not mind waiting.

The woman to my right was perhaps in her fifties—it was hard to tell. She was a large woman, though of moderate weight, tall and broad-shouldered, muscular, and dressed in such workaday clothes that her purse seemed incongruously feminine: plain pants and sturdy shoes, and a T-shirt with some message on it that I eventually identified as pro European Union. Her hair was short and curly and rather disordered, pressed down in one part and standing up in another. She wore glasses of no particular style, and these gave her a somewhat serious or studious look.

What drew my attention first, and then repeatedly, was

the speed with which she was eating. She had ordered some kind of a chicken dish—chicken drumsticks with a pile of white rice. I later decided that it had to be one of the specials of the day, available for a good price. All her motions were quick, perhaps twice the normal speed of a person consuming a restaurant meal, even one at an inexpensive lunch place. She manipulated her utensils, wielded her knife and fork, one in each hand, constantly, industriously and busily, her elbows out to the sides. She chewed fast and swallowed fast. Some of her motions were neat, as when she cleaned a drumstick of its flesh and placed the bone at one edge of her plate, alongside another bare bone. But sometimes she overshot her aim, so that rice spilled off the edge of her plate. She would quickly reposition a drumstick to present a different angle for cutting, and occasionally give the plate a little spin to reach another drumstick or gain better access to the pile of rice. Spin, stab, slice, open mouth, receive forkful of food, chew, swallow; spin, stab, slice, etc.

After I had watched her eat for a few minutes, I noticed that she had, to her right, in front of her, facing her, and increasing my sense of the urgency with which she was eating—or more than urgency, the frantic haste—a small round-faced travel alarm clock. And yet, through the course of her lunch, she did not otherwise seem in a hurry to finish her meal and leave the place. She paused sometimes to read her newspaper, and later to make a note in a notebook.

Her newspaper was folded and laid on the table in front of her. She looked at it from time to time, or picked it up and refolded it. I had my own paper, though it was a different kind of paper, a literary weekly, also folded and laid where I could read it, though I did not read it, being too interested in the people around me. She and I may have been sitting on the same banquette that ran the length of the wall, because I remember that she had room to keep her purse next to her, and so did I. Beyond her, the row of little tables continued as far as the partition.

I noticed her purse because at one point she pulled a notebook out of it and then began searching through it for a pen, again moving hastily, now scrabbling wildly in its depths, pulling it closer to her, lifting it onto the table the better to search. When she did not find a pen, she looked up and around at the people near her, including those in my direction, and asked us all generally if anyone could lend her a pen. I hesitated, waiting for someone else to offer. I had been writing in my own notebook, though I had put it and my pen away. I did not want to lend her a pen, even though I had more than one.

The man who had been reading the newspaper, and who was by then, though still silent, sharing a dessert of palatschinken with his wife, eating from the same plate, lent her his pen, passing it to her by way of an elderly woman who was sitting across from me. Once she had the pen, my fast-paced neighbor bent far over, bringing her near-sighted eyes close to the page, and began writing, again with quick motions, in her notebook.

The elderly woman across from me had made her way to my little table because the other seats in the restaurant were by now all occupied. She had asked me if the seat opposite me was free, and I had nodded and said it was. I probably said only, "*Ja*," because although I could understand some of what was said to me in German, I could not reply in very elaborate or idiomatic sentences.

The elderly woman had ordered her meal, which I saw, when it came, was the same plate of chicken drumsticks and rice as my neighbor to the right. My new tablemate, before her meal arrived, watched soberly and intently as I ate my own meal, which had at last been brought to me, not long after she had sat down. She watched me for a little while and then asked me, still soberly and intently, whether that was a slice of ham or a slice of fish. I said it was fish and then, remembering the words on the menu, I reproduced them fairly accurately, I thought, specifying that it was smoked salmon. She thought about that while she continued to watch me eat, and then she asked, still unsmiling, and not as though she were making polite conversation but rather as though she simply wanted certain information, how did I suppose they smoked the salmon. I barely caught the meaning of her question, and I forgot—though I remembered later—how to say the useful and emphatic phrase I often overheard people saying on this trip, which was "*Keine Ahnung!*" meaning "No idea!" so I merely smiled and shrugged to indicate that I didn't know.

Our conversation died, her meal came, and she in turn lowered her head and tackled her rice and chicken, at a steady speed but in a methodical, tidy manner.

For a time, I felt that we five, in that corner of the restaurant—the silent but contented married couple, who had now finished their palatschinken and returned to their former activities, he reading his newspaper, she gazing at the room; my new table partner with her pale wrinkled face, her little bun of white hair, her somber curiosity; my large-framed energetic neighbor to the right with her firmly-planted feet, her wheeling elbows, and her alarm clock; and I—were an odd group, and in our variety reminded me, more than anything, of a group of the more harmless patients on a mental ward at mealtime, each with his or her own difficulty in the face of the food. I, of course, in such a group, I thought, would be the least incapacitated, or the sanest, though somewhat excessively busy taking notes about the others.

In time, the fast eater—who, for all her speed, had not outpaced the elderly woman—was finished with her lunch, and the elderly woman was also finished, and they both paid their bills. The elderly woman handled the transaction easily and decisively, naming the amount the waitress should take—a little more than the price of the meal—and the fast eater in a state of slight confusion, holding the money on her palm and letting the waitress help her to count it out. My elderly tablemate slipped unobtrusively into her beige raincoat, picked up her purse, and left the restaurant quietly while most of my attention was on my fast neighbor.

Her preparations to leave were quite elaborate, especially compared to those of my tablemate. After standing up from the banquette and moving out into the room, where there was more space for maneuvering, she quite openly and unselfconsciously zipped and fastened her pants, which she had evidently undone for greater comfort while eating. She then stowed her clock and notebook in her purse—she had earlier returned the pen, passing it to me to give back to the peaceful married man. She next started off down among the tables to return her newspaper to the shelf at the far end of the room but turned back when she remembered that it was her own. Nearly back at her table, she stopped the manager and said something to her and remained standing there waiting. The manager went away and came back with a datebook and they conferred over the pages. Perhaps the manager was reserving a table for the next day, though that seemed odd to me in a casual lunch place such as this. Or perhaps they were making some other kind of appointment, though I couldn't imagine what that would be. She then went into one of the restrooms, whose doors were opposite our tables, and came out again. Finally she put on her rain jacket and took up her purse, nodded left and right to her neighbors, saying goodbye, made her way back down among the tables, and disappeared out the door.

I was left wondering about the open datebook, and the appointment, and more generally about her. What was she doing? Who was she? Did she live here in this town, or was she visiting? She seemed very familiar with the place, she did not seem like a visitor, she was not dressed like a visitor. I thought she was a local person who liked to eat lunch here. And yet the manager and waitress did not seem to know her, as they would have known a regular customer. Or perhaps they knew her but preferred to keep their distance from her.

The quiet couple still sat quietly, now both looking out into space, still blandly pleasant and calm.

After a long afternoon of walking up and down more streets, venturing into the front halls and up the stairs of small old apartment buildings that interested me because of their age or their conformation, climbing up and then back down the steps cut into the rock face leading to the Capuchin monastery, crossing the river again and walking on uphill through the Domplatz and into the vast Residenzplatz, where a Nazi bookburning had taken place, stopping to read the plaque, which included a good quote from Heinrich Heine about burning books, running under a sudden downpour to the archway of the museum of the city of Salzburg, entering the museum to see the famous 19th-century painted panorama of the city, buying, in the gift shop, a piece of reddish salt rock from the Salzburg mine, continuing downhill to Mozart's birthplace and visiting every room of every floor of the house, pausing to stand for a while in the room in which he was born, returning over the river to see the larger and grander house in which his family had lived later in his childhood, walking through the vast ballroom of that house, in which dance classes had been held, I was tired as evening approached. The museums were closing, dinnertime loomed, and I needed to make the important decision of where to eat.

Some acquaintances with whom I had been sitting the evening before, late into the night, on a cafe terrace that looked out over a broad, dark leafy street of massive nineteenth-century residences, had made several suggestions, each accompanied by a good deal of discussion, and I had written them all carefully down. But now I was tired, and my mood was not exalted, as it had been the night before, and I no longer had the ambition or resolve to walk back into the heart of the city and find one of those restaurants. I wanted to return to my hotel, which was some distance away in the opposite direction, and I wanted to rest and then stay there.

Perhaps my acquaintances had told me the hotel restaurant was itself quite good, or perhaps when I returned to the hotel, tired, to await the hour for dinner, I looked at the menu posted outside the door to the restaurant and decided it would be good enough. In any case, after resting in my room for a short time, until the earliest moment I could go down, I went back down and into the restaurant.

But there, I found that the main dining room, at the back, had been reserved for a large tour group. I was told, as I stood by the long bar of the restaurant, that I could still eat in the restaurant, but I would have to eat there in the barroom—the ample room in which we were talking. I looked around. It had a mirrored wall, wooden chairs, many wooden tables covered with red-and-white-checked tablecloths, and a row of windows opening on the street. It did not seem as calm and comfortable as the room I had imagined, but as long as I could eat from the regular dinner menu, I did not mind. I thought it might even be interesting. I sat down at a table against the mirrored wall and facing the entrance, where I could see the whole room. I took out the same literary weekly I had had with me at lunch, and I settled down to enjoy the peaceful interval of waiting, first, to order a drink, and then for the drink to come, and then for the food to come, leaning back against the comfortable padded banquette and resting my tired legs.

Soon I had my glass of white wine and had ordered the appealing and surprising item I had found on the menu—a fennel risotto. I read my paper, looked at the others settling at their tables, and watched the doorway, where the tour group was now coming in. They were filing across the room toward the door to the main dining room, which was near me beyond a cabinet holding silverware and napkins, and as they entered, almost every member of the group looked straight across the room in my direction and stared seriously and critically at me. I began to wonder—was it something about my appearance? No, after all, it was not me—they were looking at themselves in the mirror above my head.

My risotto was slow in coming because of the service demands of the tour group, but at last, once they were embarked on their own meal, it came, and I was well into eating it, and finding it very good, when two more people entered the room—two women. To my great surprise, one of them was, in fact, my fast-eating neighbor from lunchtime. How could this have happened? What were the chances of this happening? Salzburg was not a small town. Where had she been all afternoon, and what had she been doing?

She had not changed her clothes: She was dressed just as she had been when she left the other restaurant at lunchtime—in the short rain jacket and the pro-EU T-shirt. Her companion was a younger woman in a red sweater, with a ponytail of dark hair, who looked rather glum at first but who, I saw later, though her back was to me, talked animatedly enough during their meal. They found a table not very far from me, settled in, and ordered drinks, salads, and what looked like the same fennel risotto.

The fast eater ate fast again, and stopped now and then, as she had during lunch, to blow her nose into a large white handkerchief, with the same loud noise as earlier. But now, while she ate, she was talking in what seemed to be an exuberant and spirited way, though fast, and occasionally laughing.

I asked myself the same questions I had asked at lunchtime, along with some others—did she live here in town? If not, why was she so casually dressed? But if so, why was she eating out twice in one day? Who was her friend? Not a daughter, clearly. The fact that she was in the same restaurant as I, once again, was something I could not explain. Clearly, she liked the same sort of restaurant I liked, but that was not enough to explain the coincidence.

Well into the meal, the two were joined by a stout, older man who gave them each a handshake rather than a kiss. He did not eat, but sipped a coffee as the three of them talked. Well, who was he? A friend? A lawyer? The fact that she was eating in a convivial way with two companions made her seem to me less odd than she had seemed at lunchtime, and yet her unusual behavior of lunchtime remained a fact. This evening she did not, at least, have the alarm clock in front of her on the table. She had probably—though not certainly—not unfastened her pants.

I spent some time debating whether to speak to the waitress, who seemed to know several of the customers, and ask her if this woman was a regular customer, and if she could tell me anything about her. But I could not think how to do it. I finished my meal well before the fast-eating woman and her companions, and left the restaurant, thinking I might still come back down from my room a little later and talk to the waitress. I never did—it would have been too complicated to manage in German, and it would have appeared too strange.

Another coincidence: although my lunch and my dinner that day had been entirely different, my bill was exactly the same, down to the cent.

This was a simple story, and perhaps pointless. But I was still remembering things about the fast-eating woman the next day on the train through the mountains, headed for Zurich. I was reminded of her in part because I was again reading the stories of Peter Bichsel and because of my interest in the way he observed and wrote about the people in his world, and the way he conceived and constructed a story. I was reading his stories on the train and thinking now and then about this woman, but I was also observing the other passengers, one of them being the white-haired man across from me. He was himself like a character in a Bichsel story, such an avid reader that even as he entered the compartment he carried an open book in his hand, and he resumed reading as soon as he had sunk into his seat, his jacket still on, one foot in the aisle braced against the motion of the train.

Claim to Fame #6: Theodoric

I have at least one thing in common with Theodoric, King of the Ostrogoths. We have both taken an interest in the city of Arles, in France, and invested some of our personal money in it.

Theodoric, in the sixth century, residing part of each year in the city, gave a substantial amount of cash to the bishop, St. Caesarius, toward the founding of a convent which was to be built high on the hill at the northern end of the city and headed by the saint's sister, Caesaria.

My own contribution has been more modest. After paying, as a visitor in Arles, for a hotel room and many meals in restaurants, as well as for a few souvenirs, including post-cards, books, and some lengths of cloth, I found, after returning home, that my interest in the city was only increasing, as I read further about its history, including the history of St. Caesarius and Theodoric, and I eventually sent a membership fee of $42 to join the historical association called Les Amis du Vieil Arles, which means "Friends of Old Arles." I have continued paying my yearly dues ever since, in return for which I receive a tri-quarterly *Bulletin* containing detailed articles generally of great interest to me, on the history of the city, though, to my disappointment, the latest issue was wholly devoted to bullfighting.

Overheard on the Train: Two Old Ladies Agree

"Everything gets worse."

"Does anything get better?"

More Corrections

stet caps on Navy
delete "try to" in Eating Fish Alone
separate Loud Women from Obnoxious Man
"which," when followed by a comma, would make us think the trees are the chickens roosting
stet incorrect comma
add comma before parking lot
consider the simpler solution, just removing the lamb
add "and saves" after "collects"
add "from the household" after "discarded pieces of paper"
change "aerograms" to "aerogram letters"
add "blue" before "aerogram"
change "broccoli" and "lettuce" to typical Indonesian vegetables
(look up Indonesian vegetables)
take out little girl in blueberry bush

Dear Who Gives a C***

Dear Who Gives a C***,

Thank you for the recent shipment, which arrived promptly. I'm glad to have it. I feel good about using toilet tissue made from recycled paper, even if it does not always tear off the roll neatly and is a little coarse, though we quickly got used to that and may even come to like it. In any case, I would rather suffer a slight discomfort than be complicit in the felling of old-growth trees in Canadian boreal forests merely in order to enjoy virgin toilet paper that is softer and tears more neatly. I also appreciate what you are doing to help supply toilets to people around the world.

But may I make one request? The first shipment you sent—our first order—came in an "anonymous" cardboard box, which I preferred. The latest shipment had your company name on it. I find that a little awkward. The name may be amusing to some people, and I don't mind it—or not very much—but it's frankly embarrassing to display in the neighborhood where I live, and it's certainly not language I would use myself. In fact, the language does seem generally problematic to me, since it is rude and expresses (though I know you intend it tongue-in-cheek) an attitude of brutal indifference that is all too actually pervasive in the times we are living in. I am sure you will not change your company name, but could you please offer the option of shipping your product in an unidentified box?

Also, we like the individual wrapping of the toilet rolls, striped and polka-dotted and in such nice pastel colors. Opening the carton is like opening a box full of gifts. But if you didn't print your company name right in the middle of the paper, we could reuse it for wrapping small presents, even though it would be a little wrinkled since we are opposed on principle to ironing. Wouldn't that fit better with your idea of reusing paper rather than buying single-use gift wrap? Please consider putting your name in the corner of the wrapping, or off to the side. Thank you.

Sincerely.

Sneezes on the Train

The neat, thin, round-faced young man across the aisle from me and one seat forward sneezes. The man in the seat behind him, bald and wearing a pink striped shirt, says, "Bless you!" not loudly but very distinctly. The thin man starts, looks apprehensive, but does not turn around. Then the man in the seat behind me sneezes twice in a row, quickly. I wait for the man across the aisle to bless him, too, but he says nothing. The thin man sneezes again, but this time very quietly, carefully smothering his sneeze in both a Kleenex and a scarf, then slowly turns his head just enough to glance discreetly over his shoulder at the man behind him, who continues to remain silent. Much later in the trip, the thin man is long gone from the train, and the man behind me has been replaced by a woman. Now this woman sneezes four tiny, high-pitched, suppressed sneezes in a row, followed by a fifth. I wait, and listen. Again, the man across the aisle in the pink striped shirt says nothing. Either he has lost interest, as he sits bent over studying his screen, or he feels that one bless-you per ride is enough.

(Some of) His Drinking Habits

He likes to drink at airport bars, he likes to drink on trains, and he likes to drink at the bar at South Station and at any hotel bar.

He likes these bars, and the train, because no one knows him, and everyone is on a trip or about to go off on a trip.

He says that people form bonds at these places—but it's not personal.

The Interests of Old Age

One old lady asks us kindly after the health
of another old lady of our acquaintance,
with particular concern
for the regularity
of her movements.

The People in My Dreams

1

"What does *pension* mean?"

"Does Thomas send money home to his family?"

These were the questions asked by a plump, blowsy woman of middle age in a scrap of a dream I had last night as I began to fall asleep.

Who is this woman? Why does she—emphatic, fluffy-haired, frowning—want to know the meaning of *pension* and the habits of this mysterious Thomas? And now that I've woken up, where has she gone, with her confusion and her urgency?

2

In my dream, dozing in the afternoon, I call out a car window, trying to reach others out there somewhere, but the only one who hears me is a Norwegian man by the side of the road. He is wearing a red-checked flannel shirt, and he is pruning or clipping some shrubbery. He steps out into the road behind my car and calls after me with a frown, in Norwegian—not angrily, but reproachfully, because I have startled him.

Now where has he gone, as my dream ends? After my car passes, and my dream ends, does he go back to clipping or pruning there by the roadside, looking now and then over his shoulder at the road, toward the point where my car disappeared?

3

Someone asks me who lives here. Then I see him, the man who lives here.

I had not noticed him before, but he is close to where we are standing. He sits nearly concealed in a sort of high-backed basket chair, on this wide terrace-balcony. He is a tall man, well dressed in a tan suit and brogues. I can see by his expression that he is reserved, but calm and friendly, sitting well back in the chair, looking not at us but straight ahead, with a slight smile. He is vaguely familiar to me, as though he has appeared in a previous dream. Or maybe he only seems familiar.

4

There is a man dancing boisterously in a bar, on this side of a counter, dipping his partner far back. He is a small but muscular man, she is also small and muscular, wearing a skirt that swings over her strong calves.

Are they still dancing after I wake up?

5

On another night, this man appears just briefly: he is tall, heavyset, and balding in a T-shirt with its sleeves cut off so that his brawny tattooed arms are fully visible. He is wearing cut-off jeans, so that his thick long legs can also be seen. He is holding something like a stick or an iron bar, though he is not threatening me with it. But he does look angry, or hostile.

6

There is the person A. saw once. I was with him in the dream, as I often am in waking life, and he said suddenly, "What is *she* doing?" We were both watching something, but only he could see it, whereas I saw only white space.

Where were we, who was she, what *was* she doing? I could have asked him, after I woke up, but he had not had the same dream and would not be able to answer my questions.

7

I am trying to help an Englishman cross a small lake. He needs to reach a certain street on the other side. The Englishman is fussy and old, and clings to me in a way that bothers me. I leave him for a moment standing on the pier and walk up a gangplank into a large boat. Its gangways are full of mad and senile old people. I want to see if the old man might cross the lake in this large boat.

But my dream ends abruptly there, and so the old man is left standing on the pier, alone, perhaps even more agitated and frightened, waiting for me to come back.

8

This time, it is just a voice, intruding on whatever image I had in my mind just as I was falling asleep. It says, "How can you . . . if you know what your name is?"

9

And who is this opinionated woman who has appeared during a very brief afternoon nap and then disappeared: She is disagreeing with someone (not me), and saying, "No, you won't last an *hour* standing on a tea table!"

The Sounds of a Summer Afternoon

The sound of the riding mower a few houses away is a relentless drone. But at least it drowns out the sound of the drag strip raceway over the hill from us—an angry roar rising and then falling again over and over like constant disappointment. But the worst is when both the riding mower and the drag strip raceway fall silent. Then we hear rapid, regular shots echoing from the woods—target practice with a rifle. Or the single hoarse caw and cluck of a crow overhead. Or the whine of a mosquito close to our ear. Or the neighbor's wife's high-pitched call and scold. Or the buzz of a bumblebee stopping on a flower and then moving on—always the same note, maybe a B flat. Or the twitter of a swallow ending in a silly rattle. Or the monotonous chirp of a chipping sparrow. Or the endless babbling warble of a robin. Or the throat-clearing and dry page-turning of a person reading nearby.

Three Deaths and One Old Saying

1

A dog walking over a piece of warm pavement was electrocuted. His hair stood on end, he yelped, he ran a few feet, and he fell over dead. The vet who later examined him said his lungs were full of blood.

2

A woman of Manitoba was clinically dead for four hours, lying in a snow bank in the street without an overcoat in temperatures that dropped below minus 30 degrees. Although at the time of her discovery she had no heartbeat, she was later revived. It was found that her brain was frozen enough not to be damaged by this.

3

Another woman of the north, suffering from severe depression, smothered her child with a handful of snow.

4

Old saying: You can never be so dead that you don't hear the cawing of the crows.

True Fact

When I was young,
I once went to the Chelsea Flower Show in London
with my mother's second husband's third wife.
This is a true fact.

Wedding

The Rev. Leslie Dunton, pastor,
read the marriage at 4 p.m.

The bride was given in marriage by her father.

She wore a waltz-length
princess-style afternoon dress
of white cotton lace lined with white taffeta.
Her short veil of French illusion
fell from a bandeau of pearl-studded lace,
and she carried a white prayerbook
on which rested a cascade
of white rubrum lilies
and sprigs of white heather,
a Scottish tradition.
For something old,
she wore a pearl-and-diamond lavalliere,

a gift from her grandmother,
and carried her grandmother's handkerchief.

Mrs. James Bunch of Eugene,
was the bride's matron attendant.
She wore a full-skirted dress of polished cotton
in deep forest green
with matching bandeau headdress
trimmed in white flowers.
She carried an all-white bouquet
in colonial arrangement
of stock, carnations, and chrysanthemums.

Mr. Bunch was best man.

The bride's mother wore a dress of Dior blue silk faille,
with navy accessories.
and the groom's mother an aqua faille sheath,
with black accessories.
Both had corsages of small white chrysanthemums.

Organ music at the ceremony
was played by Mrs. Stanley Olson.

At the wedding reception,
the refreshment table was spread
with a Chinese cloth of white grass linen,
a family heirloom.
The table centerpiece was of green spider crysanthemums
and Bells of Ireland.
The wedding cake was a tiered dark English fruit cake
baked by an aunt of the bride,
Mrs. A. L. Leathers of Seattle.

The cake was cut by Mrs. Weidkamp.
The tea was poured by Mrs. Conrad and Mrs. Schuttpelz.
Miss Nancy Grant had the guest book,
and D. J. Grant served punch.

For their wedding trip along the coast,
the bride chose a suit in pale blue tweed
with red velvet hat and accessories.
She wore a corsage of white carnations
centered by a Garnett rosebud.

The bride and groom are now at home on Cal Young Road
in Eugene.

Trying to Get in Touch with Her

We haven't talked in a long time,
more than ten years, maybe fourteen—
time keeps passing and I lose track.

She's not far away.

I know she would want to hear this.
And there is so much other news by now.

She's just upstairs, what is left of her.
She used to be on the floor, in a corner of the room.
Then we moved her pretty jar to a shelf.

You'd just think there would be some way—
For a short visit at least.

Two Drunks at Dinnertime

She was a little drunk cooking dinner, and burned everything.
He was a little drunk eating it, and didn't care.

Ugly?

I'm not sure if this lamp here in this shop is ugly.
It may be ugly, but it may simply be unusual, colorful and strange.
On the other hand, everything else in this shop is ugly.
So the lamp is probably ugly too.

What I Understand

I understand a great deal, on some days I even believe that perhaps there is really nothing I don't understand, or rather nothing I would not understand if it were presented to me clearly, whatever it might be, from any discipline, from anywhere in the world, from any culture and any history. But now that I have said this, I realize it may not be true. It occurs to me that there are some things I don't understand, however hard I try, such as certain mathematical concepts, or certain institutional arrangements, or certain medical conditions, no matter how often these things are explained to me, or how clearly, and whether from my own culture or another. Sometimes, I understand them for a moment, for as long as I try hard to understand, and then, as soon as I think of something else, or go away for a while and come back, I no longer understand them. And even if they are explained to me again, just as clearly, I will continue not to understand them after a few minutes of thinking about something else. And so, after all, it is true that I am confused by certain disciplines, I stumble in a few areas, I am lost in some fields.

How He Changed over Time

He used to play the violin, but then, as his fingers thickened and lost some of their agility, he became frustrated by trying to play, and then bored by it. He put the violin away in its case for good, had the case removed to a storeroom, and, instead, invited others in to play for him and his family in the evenings. In time, this playing by others, too, wearied him with its incessant noise and he no longer invited musicians into his home or willingly listened to any music, except perhaps, at long intervals, from a distance, a patriotic march.

He used to provide what was needed in the way of food, equipment, and guides, for parties of men to go off exploring. They would bring back to him not only reports of what they had seen but also handsome artifacts, such as feathered tribal headdresses and small handmade axes and other tools. These he would display in his roomy octagonal front hall, and visitors waiting for a private audience would pass the time studying the artifacts and learning about the indigenous tribes of the country. He had had exactly this in mind, to educate the public, when he caused the artifacts to be displayed thus on the walls and in cabinets in that particular place. But then he tired of the artifacts and lost interest in what they signaled of other cultures, and no longer cared about educating the public. He had everything in the front hall taken off the walls and out of the house and sold to a museum. The bare walls, a relief to his eyes, were then to be painted gold. He no longer sent parties of men out to explore the wilderness, for he no longer had any interest in other landscapes or the wildlife or primitive peoples that inhabited them. Geography now merely confused him.

He used to import and drink fine wines from France. But then he gave up drinking alcohol and put a high tariff on imported wines. If he could not enjoy the wines, he would make them more costly for others to enjoy. More generally, although he had once admired France and studied French architecture, looking for ideas for his own house, he no longer showed any respect for that country or any European country. He felt that the French, even more than other Europeans, might possibly be smarter and wiser than he was, and that feeling caused him to turn against them.

He was over six feet tall, and stood well above most other men. He had once been lean, and he knew that others had then said of him that he had "no excess flesh." But in time he grew heavier and his waist thickened, and he inclined forward as he walked, with his eyes directed down.

He used to ride his horse on the grounds of the estate and to other estates nearby, on visits to his neighbors, and he cut a handsome figure on horseback. But over the years, as he aged, and as he grew stout, it was harder for him to mount his horse and his hands were not as strong or skillful on the reins. Riding became uncomfortable, and he began to dislike his horse, as it also now disliked him. He began to avoid the company of all animals. They paid little attention to him, and he was now a man who craved attention. They required attention and care for themselves.

Once, years before, he had commissioned skilled copies of the best paintings by the old masters, to be hung on the walls of his parlor. Among them were portraits of his three heroes, men whose writings he had read and reread: Francis Bacon, Isaac Newton, and John Locke. But after a time he became bored by the subjects depicted in the paintings, or he told his wife, in any case, that he was bored by them. Many of the paintings depicted brave men, wise men, learned men, or compassionate men; these were storied men, men of myth and fable, or men who had figured in important historic events, in addition to the great thinkers Bacon, Newton, and Locke, and he was, after gazing at them for so many years, now led inevitably to compare himself to these figures. He was now led to question his own worth as a human being, when he gazed at them, and this made him uncomfortable. He had the paintings removed and replaced by poorly executed, but very large, portraits of himself.

In this same parlor, which looked out from three French windows in a large bay toward the formal garden behind the house, which he himself had designed years before, taking a formal garden of France as his model, he used to spend the evenings playing games with his children and his wife, or listening to a performance of new music on the harpsichord, or talking in French about new political ideas with a visitor from overseas. But in time he became bored by all of these activities, too often repeated. He found that they tired him excessively, and he would go off to spend the evening sitting in a smaller room by himself.

His wife had once delighted in his company and conversation, but gradually, now, she became accustomed to his absence in the evening from the family circle. As he sat in another room, she knew, he sometimes brooded. He thought that certain people looked down upon him. He would not allow her to comfort him.

At one time, he had liked to acquire new knowledge, to feel his brain actively engaged with something unfamiliar and challenging, and for this reason he had bought or borrowed and read one book after another. He acquired knowledge not only through reading books but also through listening to the talk of well-informed men and having extensive conversations with these men, and sometimes from conversing also with women, women who had intelligent or sensible ideas, including his wife. But then he tired of new knowledge. Now he preferred to be confirmed in what he already knew, or believed he knew. And then, over time, so imperceptibly that he did not see it, what he knew changed by degrees, so that it was no longer entirely true to the facts, but was in part false—now merely, in part, a mistaken belief. But since he had not perceived the change, he did not realize this.

He had at one time spoken French fluently and took pleasure in conversing with the French. He was able, also, to read German, Latin, and Greek. But as he read less and less, and ceased to welcome foreign visitors into his house, he began to forget these languages. And as he forgot them, he also came to feel that to be so very well educated was the privilege of only a few, not the many, and he preferred to be one of the many, or to see himself as one of the many. Or, perhaps, he preferred to be one of the few, but it was now a different few, it was the few of those who were powerful, and wealthy, not those few who were also very well educated.

He was at times, in some periods of his life, very wealthy, and spent his money freely, on rebuilding his house, and adding to his gardens, and increasing his library, and buying fine things, especially clothing, for his children and wife. But he was often, also, bankrupt, and at these times would sell some of what he owned. By the time he died he would be, once again, heavily in debt.

He used to enjoy a wide variety of food from Europe, especially from France, cooked in many different ways and accompanied by complex sauces. But over time, he came to prefer certain familiar cuts of meat cooked always in the same way, and plain bread. In fact, he now preferred most of his food to be plain. He ate more sweet dishes, often the same ones, and drank sweet drinks with his meals.

He used to have one of the largest personal libraries in the country, until he found it harder and harder to read anything at all. He mixed up the letters and his eyesight began to fail. He could have worn corrective glasses, but he was a vain man and would not tolerate being seen in them, even by his family. His memory also began to fail, so that he could not keep the sentences in his head, if he tried to read. For a short time, he brought in assistants to sit with him and summarize for him what was in the books, but even this became too difficult, since he could not understand, or remember, what the young men said, even as they were saying it. They sometimes drew diagrams and pictures for him and he could understand the pictures, but many complex ideas could not be represented by pictures. He now rejected complex ideas.

At last, as the books on the shelves reminded him too

painfully of what he had lost, he came to resent them and had them removed. He owned, at that point, 6,700 volumes. He sold them to the government, and they formed the beginnings of the government's own vast library. He never went to see them there, as he no longer had any interest in libraries. His own bare shelves, once the books were gone, were a relief. He did not allow a smaller collection of books to grow in the place of the large one and occupy the shelves again. He did not, in particular, acquire a copy of *Don Quixote*, as he had earlier wished to do. Instead, he declared that the shelves were to remain empty and he directed them to be painted gold. He had come to value the color gold above all else, as representing a substance of the very highest value. He had not only his shelves and the walls of his entry hall painted gold, but also the frames of his portraits.

He once took pleasure in creating his own designs, for his rooms, gardens, and furniture, and had hired fine craftsmen to execute them. After observing the architecture of France, he had added thirteen skylights to his house and a dome to surmount it, and connected two parts of the upper floor with a mezzanine, a new thing at the time. He created alcoves in the bedrooms in which to put the beds, in order to save space. In his dining room, he devised a dumbwaiter to be fitted inside one part of the fireplace, for bringing hot food up from the kitchen below, as he had seen once in a tavern in Europe. For his study, he designed a revolving bookstand. It could hold open, for reference, five large books at a time. When he no longer read books, he had the revolving bookstand removed to a storeroom. He could have sold it to a library, but he no longer harbored kindly feelings toward any library.

He once had extensive gardens of vegetables and fruits and kept a detailed diary of crops, harvests, and yields. He would walk daily through the gardens and orchards, stopping to confer with the gardeners. But then he lost interest, and tired of walking. He stayed out of the gardens and chose not even to look at them from the windows of the house. At last, he had the gardens plowed under and seeded for lawns, and, if he needed to cross the lawns, rode over them in a small cart pulled by a servant, for fear of touching the grass with his shoes. He had also, in the meantime, come to believe that exercise was harmful and that any man had only a limited reserve of physical strength which could soon be spent.

He once said that the future of the country depended on the ability of the people to make informed decisions. He continued to believe this, but came to feel it was even more important for him to control the decisions they made, and so he decided also to control what information they received. Thus, he conveyed to them not only good information, but also, when he wished or needed to, an abundance of false information.

He once had, when he was young, ideals for the country. He had visions of what it could become, and how perfect its government and its society could be. Over time, however, he lost those ideals. They tired him. He came to embrace a different idea, one that filled him with impatience. He now saw the country as a vast and rich resource to be exploited.

He once said that what gave a man happiness was two things—tranquility and occupation. But then he came to reject tranquility as being unproductive and to prefer a state of agitation and the nervous energy of sleeplessness. Whereas he had once had many occupations, he now had few. One was to watch other men more articulate than he was engage in public debate. At least one of them had to adopt a position with which he agreed, since for him to be in disagreement agitated him more than he could bear.

As for happiness, he was almost certainly not a happy man. He was certainly not as happy as he had once been. But because he offered false information not only to others, but also to himself, he surely would have declared, if asked, that he was a happy man.

Wise Old Men

In our society, old men are not considered to be wise, but, rather, odd, eccentric, opinionated, sloppy, foolish, forgetful, stubborn, weak, confused, clumsy, etc. This old man standing in front of me in line, that old man over there trying to open the door—what a bother, get out of our way, with your slow shuffling feet and your hesitation and your uncertainty, we say. Can't you get all the way across the street before the light changes? In another society, it is different. He is an old man, they say, ask him.

Unusual Ornament

Hanging on the wall of the American home of an expatriate Chinese couple is a framed golf ball.

Why, why?

The Chinese man works in insurance. Does not play golf.

Ask, ask.

Answer: It is the wife. She is a designer of golf balls!

Ahh, ahh.

Emergency Preparation

We filled the bathtub with a few inches of cold water, in case the pump stopped working. We were afraid to fill it more than that, for fear one of the cats might fall in and drown. The cats did not fall in.

What drowned was a daddy longlegs.

No one missed him, we thought. But with insects it's hard to tell.

The Left Hand

The left hand prides itself on being more *refined* than the right hand. Yes, it is in fact a little slimmer, the knuckles are not as knobbly, and the skin is smoother. But, says the right hand calmly, think of all the work I've done that you haven't done over the years. Well, says the left, I've been there alongside you all the way, helping. But think of all the things you can't do that I can, says the right. Think of all the skills I've developed.

The left hand hasn't worked as hard as the right. It is usually the assistant. It braces and steadies the carrot while the right hand cuts. It braces and steadies the notebook while the right hand writes. It braces and steadies the whole body in a crouching position while the right hand scrubs the floor or digs in the flower bed. True, there are some things they do together in a balanced way. For instance, they play the piano together. But even here they are not equal: the left hand is quite effective at repeating a chord over and over, even a broken chord, but not very nimble in the 16th-note passages, not nearly as nimble as the right. The right hand points that out.

Now the left hand is hurt. Its fourth finger has always been especially weak and can't move very independently. The left hand has always been frustrated and ashamed of how clumsily it plays. Though in fact, the left hand is aware that by the highest standards, the right hand's 16th notes are not all that even or fast.

The right hand apologizes. It says, Yes, sometimes you catch a thing that I've dropped. And you do turn off the water when I leave it on by mistake.

Don't forget, says the left hand, still hurt, that you may be more skilled than I am with a knife, but the other day you sliced some skin off the tip of my thumb. And remember that once you cut through my little finger so deeply that I've permanently lost some feeling in it. That was years ago, says the right hand. Still, says the left. I'm the one you injure when you stop paying attention—I don't think you really care.

Both hands wear rings. The left hand is proud that it wears a ring all the time and that the ring is gold. But the right hand is proud that it wears a ring on special occasions, and that the ring was bought in Europe.

Some things they do together with equal skill, such as washing each other in the basin—though it is true that the right hand is the one who reaches across for the soap while the left hand draws back, out of the way. And, says the right hand, when we are rinsing, I make sure there is no soap under your ring. True, says the left hand, but on the evenings when you have worn your ring, I remove it while we are washing, I rinse it, I hold it while you dry it, and I put it away in the wooden box. But, says the right hand, I open the box. True, says the left hand. It is tired of arguing. It says to itself, Don't we work together? Don't we learn from each other? The right hand could keep going, it is full of ideas and energy for more argument, but the left hand is silent, so that is the end of it. For now, anyway.

Up So Late

Past midnight, house is quiet.
I have been reading for a long time.

Now here comes a tiny bug
down the page of my book.
Oh, look—I am not the only one still awake in the house!

But what are *you* doing up so late?

Your Music Selection of the Day

Today your music selection is Beethoven's familiar "Für Elise,"
an electronic version,
out of tune,
while you wait on the phone
for the busy pharmacist to return.

When We Are Dead and Gone

When we are dead and gone,
it might be comforting
to hear the quick knock on the door
and the voice from the far side saying,
"Hóusekéeping!"
though we won't be able to open the door.

Acknowledgments

Grateful acknowledgment is made to the editors of the following publications, in which these stories first appeared, sometimes in slightly different form and/or with different titles:

American Short Fiction: "Conversation at Noisy Party on Snowy Winter Afternoon in Country," "Conversation at Noisy Party on Snowy Winter Afternoon in Country (Short Version)"; *Barzakh*: "Neighbor Stare"; *Big Big Wednesday*: "England," "That Obnoxious Man," "Those Loud Women," "Trying to Get in Touch with Her"; *Black Clock*: "When We Are Dead and Gone"; *Bomb*: "Forgetting Caen"; *Bomb* broadside insert: "Father Has Something to Tell Me," "Crepey"; *Conjunctions*: "On a Winter Afternoon," "Enemies," "Caruso," "A Woman Offering Magazines," "Fun," "The Investigation," "In Truth," "Her Selfishness," "Feeling Small"; *Electric Literature*: "On Sufferance"; *en bloc*: "True Fact," "Betrayal (Tired Version)," "Emergency Preparations"; *Epiphany*: "Letter to the Father," "Marriage Moment of Annoyance—Speculations," "Your Music Selection of the Day," "Wedding"; *Faultline*: "A Friend Borrows a Better Shopping Cart," "Gramsci," "Helen's Father and His Teeth," "Interesting Vegetables," "Recurring Turnip Problem"; *The Financial Times*: "Winter Letter"; *Five Points*: "Letter to the U.S. Postal Service Concerning a Poster," "How Sad?"; *FourTwoNine*: "Master Builder," "Personal Announcement"; *f(r)iction*: "On the Train to Stavanger"; *Gesture*: "The Afternoon of a Translator," "Our Network," "What I Understand," "Conversation Before Dinner," "Late Afternoon," "Marriage Moment of Annoyance—Mumble," "Unusual Ornament"; *Gigantic*: "Overheard on the Train: Two Old Ladies Agree"; *Granta*: "Spelling Problem"; *Guest*: "More Corrections"; *Gulf Coast*: "Not Yet Ring Lardner," "The Joke," "The Other She"; *The Halloween Review*: "Three Deaths and One Old Saying"; *The Happy Hypocrite*: "Here in the Country," "Ugly?," "The Interests of Old Age"; *The Harlequin*: "An Explanation Concerning the Rug Story," "Sunday Night at the Summer Cottages," "Up So Late"; *Harper's*: "Pardon the Intrusion" (excerpt); *Litmus*: "A Person Asked Me About Lichens"; *London Review of Books*: "Dear Who Gives a C***"; *McSweeney's Quarterly*

Concern: "Fear of Loose Tongue," "Opportunistic Seed," "Two Mayors and a Word," "Multiple-Choice Question Posed by Stranger in Pamphlet"; *Miracle Monocle*: "On Their Way South on Sunday Morning (They Thought)," "Claim to Fame #1: Ezra Pound"; *New Flash Fiction Review*: "Conversation in Hotel Lounge"; *The New Statesman*: "Old Men Around Town"; *The New Yorker* online: "Everyone Used to Cry"; *The Paris Review*: "After Reading Peter Bichsel," "Improving My German," "The Left Hand," "Tantrums," "What You Could Get for Your Turnips," "Three Musketeers," "An Incident on the Train"; *PEN America*: "The People of My Dreams"; *Ploughshares*: "Unhappy Christmas Tree," "Caramel Drizzle," "End of Phone Conversation with Verizon Adjustment Person," "Hands on the Wheel," "Second Drink"; *Posit*: "Claim to Fame #2: Karl Marx and My Father," "Claim to Fame #3: June Havoc," "Claim to Fame #4: Sally Bowles," "Claim to Fame #5: Rex Dolmith"; *Tweed's*: "Pearl and Pearline"; *Tyrant*: "Our Young Neighbor and His Little Blue Car," "(Some of) His Drinking Habits," "Fear of Aging"; *Vassar Review*: "My Briefcase," "The Talk Artist," "Criminal Activity in Colonial Williamsburg," "Democracy in France, in 1884"; *Virginia Quarterly Review*: "Community Notice: Example of Redundancy," "In a Hotel Room in Ithaca," "Not Much to

Tell," "Sneezes on the Train," "A Moment Long Ago: The Itinerant Photographer," "Egg," "Just a Little," "Two Stories About Boys."

The following were first published in *Plume Poetry* anthologies #3, #5, #6, and #7: "Heron in the Headlights," "Sabbath Story #1: Circuit Breaker," "Sabbath Story #2: Minyan," "Woman Goes to Racetrack Owner," "The Sounds of a Summer Afternoon," "A Brief News Story from Years Ago."

The following were first published in different issues of *Plume Poetry* online: "Lonely (Canned Ham)," "Two Drunks at Dinnertime," "Poem of Greeting," "Father Enters the Water," "But It Is the First Stage in His Construction Work," "Aging," "Unfinished Business," "Claim to Fame #7: A. J. Ayer," "Claim to Fame #8: On the Way to Detroit," "Claim to Fame #9: In Detroit."

"Mature Woman toward the End of a Discussion About Raincoats over Lunch with Another Mature Woman" was first published in the anthology *Funny Bone: Flashing for Comic Relief.*

"New Things in My Life" also appeared in the Belgian magazine *Deus Ex Machina*, in a Dutch translation by Willem

Groenewegen. "Egg" was also published in Dutch translation in *Deus Ex Machina*. "An Ant" and "A Woman Offering Magazines" were also published in Dutch in *Liter*.

"On the Train to Stavanger" also appeared in *Best Small Fictions 2019*.

"Our Strangers" also appeared, in a shorter form, in my early collection *Story and Other Stories* and in yet a different form, in a Swedish translation by Malin Bylund Westfelt, as a chapbook in a boxed set of novellas published by Novellix. The story has grown over time.

The writing style and approach to storytelling in "Incident on the Train" were inspired in part by the swift, neat, and compulsively told stories of Stephen Dixon and Ron Carlson. The style and sensibility of "Unhappy Christmas Tree" benefit from the influence of Russell Edson, whose works have been excellent examples, over the years, of the very short and, sometimes, boldly absurd story.